PROMISE ME

A SECOND CHANCE ROMANCE

WILLOW WINTERS

AUTHOR'S COPYRIGHT

Hard to Love
Desperate to Touch
Tempted to Kiss
Easy to Fall

This Love Hurts

Merciless World Spin Off

It's Our Secret

Standalone Novels:
Broken
Forget Me Not

Sins and Secrets Duets:
Imperfect (Imperfect Duet book 1)
Unforgiven (Imperfect Duet book 2)

Damaged (Damaged Duet book 1)
Scarred (Damaged Duet book 2)

Willow Winters
Standalone Novels:

All I Want is a Kiss
Tell Me To Stay
Second Chance
Knocking Boots
Promise Me
Burned Promises
Forsaken, cowritten with B. B. Hamel

Collections

Don't Let Go
Deepen The Kiss
Kisses and Wishes

Valetti Crime Family Series:
Dirty Dom
His Hostage
Rough Touch
Cuffed Kiss
Bad Boy

**Highest Bidder Series,
cowritten with Lauren Landish:**
Bought
Sold
Owned
Given

**Bad Boy Standalones,
cowritten with Lauren Landish:**
Inked
Tempted
Mr. CEO

SYNOPSIS

"Promise me you'll love me after this?" Those were the words I asked my first love on a high school date.

"Always, Vi," he told me before crushing his lips against mine.

I gave him a part of me I can never get back that night. Even worse, I gave him my heart.

That was four years ago. Back when I was young and naive. Back when I thought we'd always be together.

He dumped me right after graduation and left me to join the military. He said I shouldn't wait for him; it didn't matter that I wanted to. I would have waited for him forever, but he threw me away and left me here in this small town.

Now he's home and says he wants me back. Second chances don't work in love. No matter how much I wish I could erase what's happened since he's been gone... no matter how much I think of falling back into his arms...

PROLOGUE

VIOLET

I shift a little on the blanket as the sounds of crickets from the woods behind us get a bit louder. We're alone out here on the outskirts of the state park. I can hardly breathe in this strapless lace dress, and it's awkward sitting on the ground with it riding up so high. It's the prettiest one I have though, and the most revealing. It's not that it's too tight, although it feels as if it is.

Tonight's the night.

I peek up to my right at Hunter and give him a shy smile, feeling the warmth of a blush flood my cheeks. My heart swells, although I'm still a bundle of nerves. He looks so handsome even in his simple faded jeans and white tee shirt.

My lungs fill with the scent of his cologne. He smells so good. He's never worn it before. He knows tonight is different, too.

We've been dating for almost a year. We're high school sweethearts. A full year. I'd say it's my longest relationship, but it's my only one ever. And I never want another. I want to be his, and only his. Tonight I'm taking a leap of faith.

I know when we graduate in three months, it's going to be hard. He's going into training, and I'll be going to college. I lace my fingers between his; his hand is resting on my bare thigh. He looks down at me and clasps my hand while giving me a sexy smile. We're going to make it work though. He's my one and only. And I'm his.

His arm is wrapped around my waist and we're seated on the edge of the blanket. My bare toes sweep along the grass as he pulls me closer to him. The spring air is a bit chilly at night, and goosebumps form down my arm. I didn't bring a jacket. A small shiver runs up my shoulders and I curl up against his hot body. A deep chuckle rises up his chest. I love that sound. I love it when he laughs like that. He rubs his hand up and down my arm, warming me.

I lay my cheek against his hard chest and put my hand on the lower part of his stomach, against his shirt. My heartbeat picks up and I feel like I can barely breathe. My fingers dip down a little lower. The tips brush along his bare skin.

My breath stills in my lungs. I'm going for it. I bite down on my bottom lip and clench my thighs as arousal pulls between them. I slip my hand a little lower, past the deep "V" of his hips, and they just barely push into the waist of his jeans when his hand wraps around my wrist, holding me still. I can feel the coarse hair below.

"Vi," he says, and there's a hint of admonishment in his voice.

My heart squeezes in my chest. I know we shouldn't, and he's never pressured me, but I want him. I want this to happen. And I know he does, too.

2

"Hunter." I feel brazen as I keep my fingers dipped below his waistband and meet his gaze. His eyes heat with a fire I've seen before.

"I know you want this," I barely whisper. In the past, he's been quick to pull away, but this time he only holds me tighter.

He closes his eyes and speaks just above a murmur, "Vi." My name slips between his lips with a reverence I've never heard before. His grip on my wrist loosens and I pull away, but only to place my hand... down there, against him. My eyes widen slightly. I've never felt his dick before. I've never even seen one. I wasn't expecting it to be so big, or so hard.

My hearts stutters in my chest and my pussy clenches around nothing. My hand itches to pull away, but instead I push it harder against his cock, to feel more. My fingers wrap around his length as best they can in this awkward position. I can feel everything in me pulsing with need.

"Violet," he breathes my name.

In an instant, he looks back at me and moves me to his lap, pulling me away. I wrap my arms around his neck, feeling vulnerable and desperate for his love. It will crush me if he denies me. *Please, don't.*

"I'm ready, Hunter." I stare into his gorgeous green eyes. I swallow thickly and keep my voice as even as I can as I say, "I love you, and I want you to know it."

"I already know," he whispers as he brushes my hair out of my face. It tickles as it moves over my shoulder, and another shiver runs down every inch of my body. This time it hardens my nipples as his lips graze the sensitive skin of my neck, just below my ear. His hot breath forces a small moan from my lips.

"I love you, Vi." I close my eyes as he plants open-mouthed kisses up my neck and along my jawline. I love it when he says my name. He's the only one who calls me that.

I believe him. I believe he loves me. And I know I love him.

He pushes his lips against mine. There's a tenderness that I haven't felt before. I reach up and spear my fingers through his hair. I part my lips and press my body against his.

I want him to know how much I need him. *All* of him.

I kiss him with desperation. He groans deep in his throat and splays his hand on my back, lowering me to the blanket. He breaks our kiss only for a moment to look down at me.

My lips are parted, and my eyes are half-lidded with lust.

When he lowers his lips to mine and his hands travel up my dress, slipping it up past my thighs, I know this is really going to happen.

"Promise me you'll love me after this?" I sound weak, but in this moment, I need his reassurance.

"Always, Vi," he says before crushing his lips against mine.

I gave him a part of me I can never get back. Even worse, I gave him my heart.

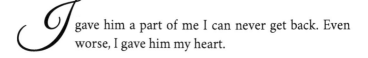

... *T*hat was four years ago. Back when I was young and naive. Back when I thought we'd always be together, and that he hadn't lied. He dumped me

4

right after graduation and left me to join the military. He said I shouldn't wait for him; it didn't matter that I wanted to. I would have waited for him. I was a fool. It was all a mistake.

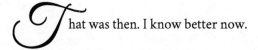hat was then. I know better now.

CHAPTER 1

VIOLET

I take a deep breath and exhale slowly as I push the glass door to the convenience shop open. The bells above my head chime and Marcy gives me a bright smile from behind the cash register on the small counter to the left. She's an older lady; I've known her most of my life. She doesn't make a move from her seat and barely looks up from behind her thick, dark-rimmed glasses. Her eyes wrinkle as she smiles slightly and returns to watching the small television behind the counter.

Just like everyone else in this town, she's content going through life with the same comfortable routine. For her that means sitting behind the register. This store is small, with only a few aisles to my right, and the counter to my left. I give her a small smile in return, though my heart's not in it and I resume walking the few steps to get what I came here for.

It has been such a long day. I look like crap, and I know it. I'm in my penguin flannel pajama pants and a long baggy sweater. It's my favorite sweater though, especially on these grey rainy days. The sleeves come down over my hands, and for some reason it makes me feel more comfortable. And I always wear these bottoms when I'm sick. They make me feel better, or at least I like to pretend they do.

I don't have an ounce of makeup on. I have bags under my eyes to prove I've had no sleep at all in the past few days. This is the first time I've been out of my little apartment in days, and I'm going right back home as soon as I can. Fall colds are the absolute worst.

I sniffle a little as I walk down three of the four aisles in the small store to get to the row with the cans of chicken noodle soup. I may be miserable, but I know I'll feel better after a hot bowl of chicken noodle. I'm in need of comfort food.

My mama never made home-cooked soup, but the stuff in the can worked for me when I was little, and it'll work for me now. It's a bit more expensive here in the convenience shop, but it's Sunday so the grocery store's closed down. Most everything's closed down, including my bakery.

I'm sure people will be talking about me coming out like this, the extensive rumor mill being one of the main drawbacks of small-town life. Mama's phone will probably be ringing before I even get home. Marcy may look like she's an innocent old lady, but all of the people in this town live to gossip.

But they can all get bent. I just need my soup and some cough medicine, and I'll be on my way.

I sigh at the simple thought. I need way more than soup. I need to get back to work.

I can hardly afford the part-time help from April and Nicole, two high school girls I'm paying to work the registers and help me in the evening. Everything else I'm doing on my own, and it's really taking its toll on me. Plus I've had to close the bakery for the last week since I've been sick.

It's hard work running your own business; there's so much more to it than I originally anticipated. I can't keep doing this on my own for much longer. And with one of the ovens broken, and none of the commercial grade mixers working, I'm struggling to meet product demands.

I close my eyes and push those negative thoughts away. I'm doing everything I can. It's going to work out. It has to. I just need that damn loan from the bank.

I push that thought down, too. I can't think about it now, or I'll be sick for an entirely different reason.

Right now, I just need the chicken noodle soup I'm holding in my hand, and my penguin PJs.

I'm not paying much attention when I hear the bells chime above the door and Marcy squeaks a slightly flirtatious, "Hi there," at whoever walked in. Marcy may be old, but she's not dead.

I stifle a huff of a laugh at my own little joke. At least there's a hint of a real smile on my lips now.

I turn around carelessly, ready to go to the counter where the meds are lined up in front of the register so I can grab the cough syrup and check out. I look up and start to yawn as I try to take a step forward, but my mouth slams shut and my feet stay bolted to the floor.

My heart does a flip and flutters in my chest as I catch a glimpse of Hunter.

Like… *Hunter* Hunter. My lungs stop moving and I quickly hide behind the aisle, nearly knocking bags of chips off the shelf. My heart hammers, and I have to blink a few times. He's here. *He's back.* My throat closes with intense emotion. He can't be back.

I barely peek around the corner, very much aware of how awful I look.

It's him. He's not a boy anymore. He's come back from overseas as a man.

And a badass one at that. I heard he's a sharpshooter now. Or was. I wouldn't know, since I did my best to stay far away from anyone who uttered his name. I had to.

Now he's home. I can't believe it. I seriously cannot believe my eyes. If he was home, someone would have told me.

It's a small town, and people talk. They sure as hell talked when he broke my heart and left me. But I've been sick and stuck inside for days while I recover from this bug.

I try to calm my racing heart and breathe easy, taking in the sight of his simple white tee shirt that's snug over his broad shoulders and corded muscles. He's always been tall, but his ripped muscles give him even more of a dominating presence. He has the same handsome face with a touch of stubble that has my fingers itching to touch him.

His hair is short on the sides and a little longer on top. I could spear my fingers through the top and just barely grab onto it. It's loosely styled so it looks a little messy, like he just rolled out of bed looking like a sex god.

I search his body for every little change. And there's a lot to look at. His muscles, his tattoos, his scars.

A soft sigh escapes my lips as I remember how those arms used to hold me. My chest fills with a comforting warmth.

His dog tags clink together as he turns slightly to the right.

I suck in a breath with wide eyes and quickly duck back. I hide behind the loosely filled shelves, praying he didn't see me. My heart races with anxiety, and my blood heats.

I can't believe Hunter's back.

He left me four years ago after high school graduation with a broken heart, taking a piece of me with him that I could never get back.

He ruined my reputation.

He shattered my trust in men.

And now he's back.

CHAPTER 2

HUNTER

*T*his town hasn't changed a bit.

I drive slowly through the main strip, looking at the too-familiar buildings. Since I've been gone, very little has changed in the landscape. A new diner at one end of town, a gas station at the other.

But Hallow Falls looks about the same. It feels just like it did when I was younger. Younger and dumber, maybe.

Hallow Falls may not have changed much, but I have.

The sudden wave of nostalgia that comes over me is bitter-sweet, almost painful. After everything I left behind here, only to come back four years later empty-handed, it's all a little overwhelming, to say the least. I feel like I've traveled back in time. Back before I ever enlisted in the Navy, before I ever thought about becoming a SEAL.

When my hands were less blood-soaked.

I frown at the steering wheel of my truck, trying to focus on driving to the store. Focus on the errand. But the images play through my head as I slow down at the stop light. The rain pounds against the metal roof of the truck, and logically I know it's just drops of water, completely harmless, but for a moment I can easily hear the ricochet of bullets and the smattering of gunshots in its place.

My heart beats faster, and my grip tightens on the steering wheel as though it's my gun. My breathing comes in even, it always does, no matter how hard my heart hammers and my blood heats. Physically, I'm still. I have to concentrate, they're all counting on me. I run my hand through my hair, trying to relax, but in my vision all I can see is the scope of the gun. Trying to find the bastards shooting bullets in our direction. The breeze from the cracked window morphs into the bullets whipping past me. I have to find them first. I can't let them live, or we'll all be dead.

A loud beep of a horn makes my eyes shoot open; my heart is beating fast, and a sheen of cold sweat is over my skin. I slowly push the metal pedal down and easily continue the drive.

I'm home. It's just rain.

My hands twist on the leather wheel and I relax my tense body, controlling my breathing and pushing away the thoughts and memories that haunt me. *I'm home. It's just rain.*

I haven't gone anywhere since I've been home. I've got enough saved up that I can take my time figuring out what I'm gonna do next. My only job has been killing people for the last few years, and now I don't know what's left for me.

I huff a humorless laugh and look out of my window at another shop that at least has a new coat of paint on it. I need to get out and start getting my shit together. I'd at least like to get the hell out of my parents' house. That was the plan

13

when I came back home. I was only supposed to stay with them while I was looking for a place of my own. But I've been hesitant to put a bid on anything. I'm worried about leaving my niece, Abigail. My chest tightens with pain; I owe it to her. The thought of leaving makes me feel like I'm turning my back on her. She's grown so much, and it's hard to believe how much time has passed.

My sister Haley hasn't asked a lot from me since I came home. In fact, a late night run to the store is pretty much the only thing she's wanted. It's the least I can do. She deserves more than that from me.

Mostly she's either been busy chasing her daughter, Abigail, around the house and tucking her in for her naps and bedtime, or she's kissing me on the cheek as she slips out of the house late at night. My parents watch her with furrowed brows and worried eyes, but she just laughs it off.

Haley's not at all like she used to be. She's not the only one. And she has her reasons. Just like I do.

So here I am, her Navy SEAL big brother, running this errand for her. While she's off having fun at some bar, I'm getting milk for Abigail's cereal in the morning.

I try not to grip the steering wheel too hard as I slow and turn into the parking lot of the convenience store. Thinking about Abbi is almost like thinking about her father, and thinking about him is dangerous for me.

Get your shit together, Hunter. He's the real reason I'm back home. And I can't stop seeing his face when I look at Abbi and Haley. It took me four years to come back. But he never will.

I left this town with a bad boy reputation and came back to

everyone looking at me like I'm some war hero. And I may be, but I don't feel like one. I'm not a hero. I failed when it really mattered. Nothing can take that back.

There are only a few cars parked in the rain-slicked lot, and I park near them as if I can blend in. My shoes squeak on the wet pavement as I walk through the parking lot, head down.

When I walk in the door, I almost wince. It's bright in here, that kind of bright that only grocery stores and hospitals ever are. Antiseptic.

I look toward the checkout and see one sad old lady standing there looking bored. I almost recognize her. Something about her is familiar. But I don't know how. I don't much care either.

The lady starts and looks my way.

"Hi there!" she says, smiling at me and perking up as though she's now awake. She's wearing dark-rimmed eyeglasses, which I can see have thick lenses as I step closer and let the door close behind me, the chime of the bells sending another wave of familiarity through me.

I try to return her smile as I wipe my boots off on the mat.

I look away and try to remember why I'm even in here, but I can still feel her eyes on me and I feel a prickle of unease run down my spine. I turn away, looking to escape.

I start to head down the nearest aisle, my mind tracing back to my earlier thought about Haley. I'm worried for her, and the guilt is weighing me down. Before I can think much more on it, I glance up and stop in my tracks.

There's someone in this aisle, a dark-haired woman wearing

penguin pajamas just like the ones Violet used to have. Actually, the woman is about Vi's size, too. *My Vi.*

She was the first person I wanted to see when I came back. But I know better. Two of the three times I came home, she was away at school. I missed her. The guilt of breaking things off and leaving her never felt right. I know I loved her back then. I thought I was doing the right thing, but I didn't expect it to hurt so damn much.

The third time I came home was the last fucking time. Because I saw her. I knew she was in town, and I couldn't resist seeing her. I wanted more; no woman's ever come close to making me want her like Vi. But when I stopped by her place and looked in the window before knocking on her door, she was in another man's lap. Her arm around his neck and laughing at something while he was leaning in for a kiss.

It took everything in me not to break that fucking window. It's what I deserved, and what I should've expected. I stormed off and refused to come back home. It's been over two years since then.

My teeth grind together, and my hands ball into fists at the memory. I left her. I had no right to be jealous, but I was. I still am. She's never stopped being my Vi.

There's no way it's her standing here in front of me now, but I can't stop myself from calling her name out of instinct.

"Violet?" I say with a hint of disbelief in my voice.

She slowly turns around, although she's slow to raise her eyes to meet mine.

My heart hammers in my chest. It's *her.*

Standing there, wearing a soft cream sweater that's a bit too

16

big and those same damn pajama bottoms, like she's on her way to bed. Her dark hair is thrown up into a ponytail. Her wide blue eyes and sweetheart features are still as perfect as the first time I saw them.

Her curves are hidden by her baggy clothes, but I have no fucking doubt that she is just as hot as she was the last time I held her. Even frozen as I am, my body recognizes hers.

I'm hard as a rock in seconds, and I make no effort to hide it either. The only sound is my blood rushing in my ears and the only thing I can see, is her. There's a frisson of awareness that passes between us, a spark that can't be denied and it finally unlocks me, lets me move.

"Vi?" I say, taking a step toward her as the trace of a smile threatens to show itself. My blood heats, and all I wanna do is take her into my arms. But that look on her face is holding me back. She's not mine, and she hasn't been in a long damn time. Judging by the look on her face, she doesn't want to be, and she doesn't feel the same as I do.

She takes a step back, looking defensive. She looks... well, not surprised to see me, but wary. I straighten my back and wait for her to calm down a bit. My mouth falls open, but I close it and clear my throat, not sure of what to say.

The last time I talked to her was the day I left. The day she begged me to write to her. I wrote her so many damn letters. Still have them. I never sent a single one. I always thought my father was right to tell me to break it off with her, since I didn't want to hurt her. But looking at her now, I regret it. And I did the one thing I tried to prevent. I'd take it all back if I could.

"You're back," she says, little more than a whisper. Her eyes glass over some and she looks off to the right, her lips turned down as she swallows thickly.

The sound of her voice is so familiar to me. I let my eyes close, as the feeling of being *home* resonates throughout my being. I've been walking around Hallow Falls for three days, wondering why I feel so foreign.

But this… seeing her, *hearing* her…

I open my eyes again and she's staring at me, her mouth in a hard line. The sadness replaced with anger. My heart clenches in my chest.

"Vi," I say, wanting so badly to touch her. "Listen-"

"Do us both a favor, and stay the hell away from me," she says with a touch of venom in her voice that I've never heard from her. Her words hit me like a slap in the face. It fucking hurts.

She moves in a wide circle, edging past the chips to get around me. They crinkle as she brushes against them to avoid touching me in the slightest. It pisses me off, but that's what I get. I'm not surprised she doesn't want to hear a word out of my mouth.

"Violet," I say with a hint of a warning in my tone as my hands ball into fists, but she doesn't stop.

I follow her, but she just walks out of the store, can of soup in her hand. She's pissed. She storms off and I think about chasing her down, but I don't know what I'd even tell her. I turn to the cashier as if expecting an explanation, but she just gives me a bland smile. I watch Vi get in her car and take off. She never looks back at me.

Shit. That could've gone better.

I exhale and retrace my steps, heading for the case with the milk. All the while, though, my mind is focused on her. I open the door all pissed off and wanting to rip it off the hinges. The cold hits my face, and I welcome it. I need to calm down.

Violet Evelyn Shaw. The first and only girl I ever told that I loved, the girl who stuck by my side through thick and thin, all through childhood and the beginnings of adulthood.

The girl whose heart I fucking shredded four years ago, when I joined the Navy and left her behind.

As I pay for the milk and leave the store, I know I have to make it right. Even if she doesn't feel anything for me anymore, I don't want this bad blood between us. She's the first thing that feels right since I've been home. I want her though. I can't deny that. It's the only thing I know.

I've had years to think about Violet and everything we had together. I only left her because I thought it was the right thing to do. My own father told me not to promise her anything, so I'd broken it off, thinking she deserved better than what I could give her. I thought she'd be better off without waiting on a SEAL who might not come back to her.

I thought of her every day since I've been gone, filled with nothing but regret.

I walk out of the store, keeping my head low to avoid the rain and get into my truck wishing life wasn't this shitty. I leave the parking lot, tires squealing on the slick cement, cursing myself.

I can think whatever I want about those halcyon days, but I can't change what I did.

I drive home silently, mind in the past, back to when I ended it between us. Back when she was mine.

Now I'm home, and she's moved on. But one look at her, and I want her back. I have no idea what to do with the rest of my life, but I know I want her in it.

CHAPTER 3

VIOLET

*V*i. I keep hearing Hunter say my name over and over as I lean against my kitchen counter, staring out the balcony window into nothing. Well not my *name*, but the nickname he gave me. The one that used to make me melt into him.

That bastard can't call me *Vi* anymore.

That was something special. It meant something *more* to me. Something that he ruined.

The microwave beeps and I make my way across my small kitchen and open up the door. I cringe a bit; I need to go in and give the shop the money for the soup. I didn't even realize I'd taken it without paying until I got home. Or that I didn't get any cough syrup. I sigh heavily. I don't touch the bowl, since I don't have an appetite anymore. I'm sick to my stomach over seeing him. I'm just going through the motions.

My heart sinks in my chest. I was cold to him, and I feel awful about putting that hurt look on his face. I bite the inside of my cheek and brace myself against the counter, staring aimlessly at the corners of the tile floor.

I may have been a bit mean to him, but I have to look out for me.

He's the one who taught me that. That I have to take care of myself, and that means keeping that man at a distance.

I reach for the bowl as my cat, Boots, sprawls across the welcome mat at the balcony door. His tabby coloring nearly blends into the mat, but his paws are completely white. Thus the name, Boots. Usually when he does that, it means he wants attention and pets. That's not happening right now, Boots.

I grab the bowl and slam the door to the microwave shut, as if it's the reason I'm so pissed off and upset at the same time.

It only takes a few steps in this cramped kitchen to get to the small two-person table in the breakfast nook. I sit down and will myself to eat and stop thinking about Hunter.

But he was looking at me like he wanted me, and I've dreamed of that look so many times. I'd given up on it though. I stopped seeing his face and hearing his name. After four long years, he's back.

The spoon clinks against the side of the bowl as I stir the noodles in the broth. It smells so good. It reminds me of comfort.

I'm anything but comfortable though.

Nothing's been the same since he left. He didn't just dump me and leave. It's not that easy in a small town.

He broke up with me and left me ruined. Everyone knew I'd

given myself to him. The way we were always together. The way I let him hold me.

I was proud of it before; I loved the way he held me close as though I belonged to him. But because of that, everyone knew. And even worse, everyone talked.

I force a bite of the soup down as Boots brushes himself against my legs. I can't wallow over this. That's exactly what I'm doing, though. Seeing him was like opening a wound that had only started to heal.

To add insult to injury, the asshole I dated in college told everyone that Hunter *fucked me*, as he so delicately put it. Adam asked me if I'd done anything before, and I told him. I trusted him. Then he ran his mouth when I ended things because I didn't want to take things so fast. After that jerk I stayed away from men. Not that there are many to choose from anyway.

My cheeks burn from embarrassment. I've never been with anyone other than Hunter. In four years, I've never even wanted another man.

No one can blame me. I tried, but Hunter did ruin me.

Yet everyone in this town looked at me like I was some slut.

Tears prick my eyes, but I refuse to cry. I've done my fair share of that. I promised myself I was over him and over this damn town and their gossip.

Instead I focused on school and work.

My boss finally retired a few months ago, selling me the shop, so now I own the *Sweet Treats Bakery*.

I'm somewhat stable for the first time in my life.

And now he shows up.

I've got my apartment, my job and my cat. I don't need him coming into my life and leaving me brokenhearted again.

I take another small bite as my phone goes off on the table. My blood spikes with hope, just like it used to.

Hunter?

I grab my phone and stare at it. It's the bank.

I drop the spoon to the table, feeling absolutely pathetic. I thought I was over this! Anger rises inside of me as the phone rings again.

I take a deep breath and do my best to snap out of it. I need to answer this call. I need this loan.

But I know it's Slade calling. This late at night, it has to be him... and it has nothing to do with the money I need. He doesn't handle the lending department, but he's been calling me.

This night just keeps getting better and better.

Slade's father owns the bank in this town, and Slade's the manager. I remember the last conversation I had with him and I grit my teeth. He makes me feel so uncomfortable. I'm not sure if it's the way he looks at me, or the way he's hanging this loan over my head.

He's made it clear he's interested in a date, but I don't think I have those feelings for him. Everyone seems to loves him though. He's good-looking, with a stable job and a well-off family. I don't know what's wrong with me.

But then again, I haven't felt anything serious for any man since Hunter. I groan in frustration at the realization.

Ring. I finally answer the phone, taking a deep breath.

"Hello," I answer with a sweet, even voice.

I'm good at hiding my emotions. In a small town that talks, you learn how to smile through it all.

"Violet." Slade's voice rings loud and clear through the phone.

My eyes drop to my bowl of barely touched soup. This isn't about the loan. I already knew it, but a part of me was still hoping.

"Hi, Slade," I say, and my voice is somehow more chipper than I feel.

"Well, there you are sweetheart," Slade's deep voice comes through with a tinge of southern charm. "I stopped by the bakery, but it's still closed. Now you'd tell me if things were that bad, wouldn't you?"

I hate that there's a tone of condescension, or maybe I'm just making it up. Either way, I feel the need to bite my tongue. He continues without waiting for a response.

"I'm sure we'll have that loan for you soon, sweetie," he says with confidence... just like he did the last time.

I finally manage a response, "It's just closed for a few days while I get over this cold." I pick at a pulled thread in the tablecloth.

"Are you feeling any better? I could swing by with something to cheer you up."

I sigh heavily, hating that I'm so standoffish to Slade. He really does seem like a nice guy.

My heart clenches in my chest. It's because of Hunter. I know that's why I can't let myself even consider being with another man. I don't want my heart broken again. But I need to move on.

"Thank you, Slade. That's real sweet of you. I'm feeling much better now though." I stand up and take the bowl to the sink, tipping it and dumping the broth down the drain. It's not even warm anymore.

"Well that's good to hear. You'll be able to go out with me this weekend then? There's a bit of a get-together at Andy's for the game on Saturday. I was hoping you'd say yes this time."

There's a pause at the other end, and I know I need to answer. He's asked me a few times already, and each time I've had an excuse. The only one I can think of now is that Hunter's back.

It makes me angry. I shouldn't even consider that asshole for one minute.

I should go with Slade; it'll help me deal with Hunter coming back. I feel absolutely pathetic that one look from my high school sweetheart brings back so much pain.

But I can't deny that it's there. I'm still hurting when I shouldn't be. And I need to get over those feelings and over Hunter for good.

"Yeah, Slade," a smile that doesn't reflect my emotions at all graces my lips as I reply with what's expected from me, "that sounds nice."

CHAPTER 4

HUNTER

I pull up to Andy's, the local bar, for the Saturday night football game. It's packed, just like I remembered it being back when I was a kid and wasn't allowed in here. The front doors are thrown open to allow people to move in and out of the bar freely.

The past three days all I've done is think of Vi. I'm still working on getting my shit together and deciding whether or not I'm gonna buy that place on the lake, but I can't think straight knowing she's here. I've been trying to decide how to apologize, but I don't even know what's all gone on in the last four years. For all I know, she hates me and she's married to someone else. But I sure as shit don't remember seeing a ring on her finger.

I almost bought her one myself before my father sat me down and explained that holding on to her was wrong. It was a pale yellow canary diamond. It reminded me of sunflowers, and those were her favorite. I remember just how it looked. I doubt I'd be able to find a ring like that anymore.

As I put the truck in park and walk across the gravel parking lot to the door, listening to the crunch beneath my feet, I think about how the hell I can make my way back into her life.

One person turns from the game and notices my arrival as I step into the lively bar.

"Graves! Holy shit. What's up, man?"

I smile. There's only one person in town that called me by my last name. I stride over to him and embrace Jared with a hard smack on his back, my oldest friend since preschool. He's a little shorter than me, and he's rocking the shaved head look, but otherwise he looks just the same.

"Not much, man. I'm out of the Navy," I say casually.

"Glad to have you back!" Jared says, clapping me on the shoulder. "Let's get you a beer."

Nostalgia rocks through me, and a part of it feels good, but another part hurts. I ignore it all and push all that shit to the side. It doesn't matter anyway. What's done is done.

Jared turns and threads his way into the crowd, leaving me to follow. The football fans are densely packed in, some in chairs, some standing. We navigate around them as I take my jacket off.

I notice that he's got a smooth, shiny spot on the top of his head, a place where he's genuinely balding. It's also obvious that he's been working out.

"You start working out for Krissy?" I ask, my tone teasing. Last time I came in, they were getting hitched.

"Yeah, dude. Even when she was out to here with the kid," he says, gesturing. "I was working out every day. I gotta stay in shape for her."

I chuckle. Jared married the captain of the cheerleading squad, as pretty and blonde as they come.

"I'm glad that's still working out," I say.

My heart pains in my chest. The thought of Krissy only reminds me of Vi. I can't help but feel even more regret, knowing what they have together and that I gave that up.

We step up to the bar, and I pull out my wallet, ready for a beer. I fucking need one.

"That's not any good here," Jared says, looking pointedly at my wallet. "Put it away."

I slide him a look, and see he's serious. I slip my wallet back in the pocket of my jeans.

"Hey," Jared says to the people standing next to us. "This right here is a real American hero. A vet, fresh from war."

I keep my expression blank, but inside I'm cringing. I don't like the attention, and I don't think of myself that way. I just wanna blend back in.

"Jared…" I warn, but it's too late.

"Oh. My. God!" I hear a feminine screech from a blonde across the bar who looks vaguely familiar. "You're Hunter Graves, aren't you?" she asks as she makes her way over.

I try to identify her, but I have no fucking clue who she is. "Yeah," I finally answer. I lay my jacket on the counter as her hands grip my forearm and the little blonde lets out a squeal.

"Oh my God! It must feel so good to be home!" I look back at her and feel like an asshole because I don't remember her in the least. She must realize that by the look on my face, because she giggles a little and adds, "I'm Amy; Sean's little sister."

I remember Sean from high school, and the fact that he had a sister seems logical. Although if she is a younger sibling, she might be too young to be in this bar.

"Sean and Casey and all the guys are over there."

She grins, pointing to an all-too-familiar group in the back of the bar. I start to say that it's okay, I'm good right here without talking to them, when someone scores in the football game.

The bar goes wild, whooping and screaming. I guess the Blue Devils must have won, but I'm not really up to date with what's going on. I also don't give a fuck. I needed to get out and get a drink. I didn't realize how packed it would be though.

The bar is suddenly crushed with patrons, people looking to buy a celebratory round. A guy to my right brushes against me, leaning over the counter to get the bartender's attention. I don't think much of it. He's drunk already and probably doesn't need any more.

I see Amy as she beckons to her brother.

Fuck. I'm not up for a reunion tonight.

I look at Jared, who's busy ordering shots from the bartender. I'm not getting any help from that quarter, apparently.

Suddenly, Sean and Casey and half a dozen other guys are all over me. Still hollering, clapping me on the back.

I look at them. Sean and Casey are almost identical, with

dark hair and sort of pinched expressions, but they're pretty popular with the ladies.

"Hunter? How was the war?" Sean asks, gripping my arm. "Amy said you were like, declared a hero, or something."

I swallow thickly, but keep looking him in the eyes. It's true, I got tons of medals and accolades when I left the Navy. I don't want to talk about it though. I didn't leave a hero. Maybe to others, but not to me. You can't be a hero when your fuck up is why your team leader and squad died.

I press my lips into a straight line, unsure how to respond.

"Shots!" Jared declares, coming to my rescue. I knew I liked that fucker for a reason.

The whole group whoops again, and I turn around to find a dark shot of liquor placed in front of me.

"To Hunter!" someone suggests.

"To Hunter!" the group shouts as one.

I pick up the little glass and slam the shot, mostly to steady my nerves. Everyone cheers when they finish the shot, like they've accomplished something.

"Another round!" Casey roars.

Jared and Sean hoot appreciatively.

After another shot, I'm warm, more loose. I knew coming home would mean having to see everyone again. It's better that I just get this shit out of the way.

"Hey," Jared says, elbowing his way over to me. "You see Violet?"

"What?" I ask, forcing myself back into the present. How the fuck does he know that? I know this town talks, but I hardly said a word to her. "For a minute, the other night."

"No, man. Over there," he says, pointing.

My eyes follow his gesture, landing on the back of a brunette. I frown.

She's wearing jeans, heels, and a slinky grey top. Her dark hair is piled on top of her head in a tight bun. I let my eyes slide down to her ass, an amazing testament to her jeans. My dick twitches in my pants and I hold onto the tiny shot glass in my hand a bit tighter.

It's her alright. She chooses that moment to turn around, as if she can feel my eyes on her.

The searing look she gives me the second she recognizes me, pinning me in place. Yeah, that's her. I can feel a slight buzz from the two shots starting to kick in, and it makes me want a third.

My eyes slip down to the front of her shirt for just a second. Her tits are perfect; I remember how they felt just right in my hands, and it makes my dick harden even more. When I make eye contact with her again, she crosses her arms over her chest and flips me the bird.

I see her say something to the guy to her right, tall and dark-haired. Who the fuck is he? Her hands rest on his arm, and anger rises inside of me.

I don't like seeing her with another man. The memory of her on some asshole's lap comes back to the surface, and I grit my teeth and nearly break the fucking shot glass in my hand.

He turns to her so that his face is visible, and I see that it's Slade White. Apparently she must be close with the former varsity soccer captain, because he moves his hands around her waist.

My jaw clenches, but she gives him a tight smile and tries to pry his hands away. Maybe they're not as close as he thinks, then. The corner of my lips pull up into a grin.

"Hunter," Jared says, waving a beer in front of my face.

"Thanks, man," I say, accepting the drink.

"So you saw her the other night?" he says, sipping his beer.

I nod, bringing the cold glass to my lips. "At the Cash N Carry."

"Rumor around town is that she's going out with Slade White. Or at least that he's pursuing her." He slides me a careful look. "People around town didn't have a very good opinion of her when you left."

"What do you mean?" The way he says it pisses me off. What the fuck is wrong with my Vi?

"I guess she tried dating Adam Hall. Remember him?" He waits for me to nod before continuing on. "Well, things didn't work out between them, and he spread the word that she was damaged goods. Said she'd lost her V-card to you."

I raise my brows. Not inaccurate, but it doesn't seem like something she'd want people to know. It's none of their fucking business anyway. "Is that right?"

"Yeah," he says with a shrug. "We all know different though," he looks at me pointedly, "right?"

A large group leaves the bar all at once, grumbling about saving themselves for tomorrow's game. I look back to Vi to make sure she's not leaving. She's staying put, her hands wrapped around a glass. My eyes move to the man next to her. Slade spots Sean and Casey, then me.

He smiles, the expression reptilian. I look at him with my lips pressed in a firm line, and his smile widens.

Game on, fucker.

Slade's heading my way, grabbing Violet by the hand. She looks at him, a little startled, before she looks at me.

Her blue eyes widen as he drags her across the bar and closer to me.

I can see that she's pulling on Slade's hand, trying to stop him, but he keeps moving forward. I fucking hate that she doesn't want to come over here. It's obvious. Worse than that, her hand is in his. I can't fucking stand his claim on her.

"Hunter!" Slade says, grinning. "You made it back in one piece!"

I grit my teeth. "I did."

"You must've been on an easy assignment, then," Slade says.

"Hey, hey," Jared says, butting in. "He's a Navy SEAL, okay? I'd like to see you go through the kind of training he did." I don't give a shit about Slade's opinion. So he can say whatever he wants.

The best strategy is to ignore Slade in favor of Violet. I may hate the guy, and hate that he's touching her, but he's giving me the opportunity to talk to her when it's obvious she doesn't want to. I can see Violet trying to discreetly remove her hand from his, but he's not making it easy.

I look right at Violet and wait for her gorgeous blue eyes to meet mine. "You look beautiful."

She drops her gaze and turns red.

It's quiet for a moment and I expect my heart to beat faster, but looking at her calms something in me, even if she's ignoring me. "He's giving you a compliment, sweetie," Slade says, never dropping his smile.

Vi glares at him briefly. Slade just grins at her.

"Well, I'll accept your compliment on her behalf," he says, releasing her hand and wrapping his arm around her shoulders. She looks at me once again, her eyes full of accusations and questions.

Still, she's silent. She looks away, across the bar.

"I'm gonna go say hi to Sean," she says, removing herself from Slade's embrace.

I watch her walk away, aware that Slade's doing the same thing.

"I should go," Slade says. "Gotta keep tabs on the little lady, you know?"

He gets a stony expression from me and Jared, so he moves along, smiling all the while.

"Fucker," Jared spits, disgusted. "He's just the same as he was in high school."

"Hmph."

I take another drink of my beer, watching them. From a few feet away, I can see how he dominates all her personal space, how he bullies her into accepting it.

"No fucking way she's dating him," I say, shaking my head. She's too good for him.

"I don't think she is. Not officially, at least," he says. He looks at me meaningfully. "Maybe never, now that you're back."

I keep my eyes on her as I answer back, "She won't even talk to me."

He doesn't respond and when I turn to see what he's doing, he merely smiles, then sips his beer. I ignore him and focus on my drink then back to Vi. The prospect of her dropping Slade for me is exactly what I want. I can't imagine it'd be too hard, given the way she's pushing him away.

Granted, we didn't leave off on good terms. If last night is any indication, she's still holding on to that. Jared was one of the only people who told me not to break up with Vi back in high school, that she'd wait for me. I grit my teeth, hating that I fucked up.

"Another beer?" Jared asks, bringing me back to the present.

"Yeah, that seems right," I answer. I quickly finish off the one I've got in front of me.

I try and pretend that I'm not staring at them while the bartender sets down the beers, and I wrap my hand around mine. I watch as she waits until Slade is deep in conversation with Casey, then excuses herself and heads outside.

"I'll be back," I say to Jared, who just tilts his beer at me with an amused smile.

I'm quick to make my way out to the parking lot. I push the doors open and feel the cool breeze of the night. Once it started cooling off outside someone shut the front doors of the bar. The sounds of the bar dim as the doors close behind me. The crickets are loud this time of year.

It's dark in the parking lot, but I find Violet leaning against

36

the building. Her head is down, and she's quiet. The parking lot is empty except for us, a fact I appreciate as I move toward her.

Violet looks up and sees me, spearing me with those gorgeous blue eyes. Her eyes glint with anger as I come to stand next to her.

I get close enough that I could reach out and touch her, but I don't. I know she's pissed at me, and she has every right to be, but I know my girl.

"Vi," I say.

"Shut up," she's quick to reply and it brings a small grin to my face.

"What's that?" I ask with enough humor to try to lighten the mood without pissing her off even more.

"You lost the privilege of calling me pet names a long time ago."

She crosses her arms, her eyes throwing sparks. Again, I'm surprised how calm I am. Just being close to her helps, even if she is denying me. I wanna lean in and soothe her anger too, but at this rate, she'd just slap the shit out of me.

"I just wanna talk," I say, throwing up my hands in surrender.

I know it's a lie even as I say it. I'm hard as a rock, I think it's her anger. It shouldn't turn me on, but it does. Fuck, I love it even. I don't wanna talk at all. I wanna pin her ass to the brick wall and show her who she belongs to. I want more than that though. I want *her*. I want all of her.

"You want more than you deserve," she says. "You shouldn't have come back."

She licks her lips, a nervous habit. I know I shouldn't push her further, but I do.

"What are you doing here with Slade?" I ask as if it's for her benefit and has nothing to do with me. "You're so much better than that."

"Better than Slade?" she growls. "Who are you to say?"

I step closer, so close that I could lean down and kiss her. I can smell her now, and she smells like honey and jasmine.

"You know me better than anyone," I grit out. "You tell me who I am, Vi."

She moves to slap me, quick as can be, but I'm faster. I grab her hand, just as she would've hit me.

Awareness tingles through both our bodies. I can see her shiver slightly as her lips part. Electric heat slides between us.

She looks up at me, so small and delicate. Her mouth opens, and her head tilts back. She's either readying herself to scream at me or be kissed, and I know which one I'd rather.

I don't wait a second. I lean down and kiss her, molding my lips to hers. She gasps, startled, and pulls back slightly. I move my hands to her waist, feeling her lusty hot body in my grasp and kiss her again, sliding my lips against hers, and for a second she lets me.

My fingers dig into her hips and I pull her closer. She arches her back and moans slightly.

Then she remembers herself, breaking away from me, breathless. Her small hands push against my chest and I resist for a moment. Just a moment, before pulling back.

"Don't," she warns with a shaky voice as she points her finger at me, her chest heaving and a beautiful flush now coloring her chest. She takes a step backward. "Don't you dare."

"I want you back," I tell her.

She huffs a sad, disbelieving laugh. "Right. Well, I want a lot of things, but mostly I just want to get away from *you*."

She turns around, her feet kicking up gravel as she walks away, heading for an old blue Nissan.

I follow her path and stand a few feet away as she gets into her car. I don't want her to leave, but it's not like she's going far. And I've already pushed her limits tonight. She needs time. I know her. I know my Vi. I need to give her a little space and a little time.

Now that I know where my Vi stands, I'm not stopping until she forgives me.

I won't let up until she gives me a second chance.

CHAPTER 5

VIOLET

*T*he dim daylight filters into the large windows of the bakery as I stretch my arms above my head, yawning and then letting out a weak sigh. It's late and the front of the bakery is much darker now than it was this morning. I flipped the sign to "closed" about an hour ago, and everything's all cleaned up now.

I've got to wheel this birthday cake back into the walk-in fridge and then I can get out of here, a productive day behind me. And then I have nothing left to hide behind. No more work to keep me busy and keep my mind off of what happened last night. The thought makes a touch of dread stir in the pit of my stomach. I ignore it and toss the washcloth in my hand onto the side of the large basin sink.

I take a long glance of the birthday cake for tomorrow to make sure it's perfect.

A small smile plays at my lips as I take in my handiwork. Even if my heart's not in it, my grandma would be so proud.

The thought makes me feel slightly better. She's the one who first taught me how to mold fondant and whip up the buttercream just right. She's why I thought I'd be good at this.

The two-tiered orange citrus cake is covered with a pale blue buttercream. There are white chocolate molded sea shells at the bottom, a sailboat on top with a little red flag and an "Ahoy Matey!" banner on the second tier. I think it's one of the cutest cakes I've ever made.

I'd squeal with delight if I was in a better mood. But I'm not.

I'm still in this shitty situation with Hunter and Slade, and now that it's time to close, I have to face reality.

I can't believe I did that last night. I let Hunter kiss me, I let him draw me in and make me feel something for him again. I shouldn't have. I should have my armor on when it comes to that man. But he breaks it down so easily. I'm ashamed.

For a moment, I wanted to lean into that kiss. I wanted Hunter to take me right there. To fuck me outside against the wall of the bar. Even worse, I feel like I cheated on Slade, even though we aren't even a couple. I feel like everyone was right about me.

I could feel my defenses crumbling around me. I'm pissed at myself for everything that happened last night, but when I think of Hunter...

I touch my lips and close my eyes. The spark between us was still there as he held me and kissed me like he really wanted me. I keep remembering the way Hunter leaned in and kissed me as though I was his. He wanted me last night.

He wants me.

My heart swells in my chest and my pussy heats for him, clenching around nothing. My eyes close and I feel weak, but only for a moment. I grit my teeth and shove down those feelings.

Fool me once, shame on you. Fool me twice...

I won't let that happen. I can't.

I carefully push the cart with the cake on it away from the frosting station and to the right where the double door fridge is. I have to prop the heavy door open with the stopper and then go back to the cart.

I shouldn't feel like I cheated on Slade.

I'm not his girl. I cringe remembering how he was treating me last night. I didn't expect that. I didn't want his hands on me and him hovering over me like we're an item.

But then again, I haven't really dated in so long, so maybe I'm the one who's in the wrong.

I'm so confused. I'm in a really bad mood, and somehow I just don't know how to break out of it.

My stomach churns as I kick the stopper away from the door and let it fall shut. I pull the handles slightly to make sure it's a firm seal. Like everything else in the bakery, the fridge is old.

I have too many real problems to deal with. I don't need to fall back into an old habit, whether that would be Hunter or this pity party I'm throwing myself. That's only going to make me angry at myself all over again.

I close out the register and have to hold back the self-doubt I have about continuing to run this place.

I had a great day today in terms of sales and customers. Although the money coming into the bakery is good, the bills are piling up.

I wish I was just a baker. It was better back when Mr. Mealey owned and ran everything. When he hired me, he told me the job wouldn't last long and that he was going to be retiring.

I jumped at the opportunity to own this place. I practically begged him to teach me.

I lock up the shop, thinking about one problem after another.

The keys jingle in my hands as I turn and walk back to my car, just to the right of the shop. I open the car door with a loud click in the otherwise empty, quiet air and ease into the seat, exhaustion taking over my body. Owning a small business is hard work and more difficult than I ever imagined.

I close the door, but I don't put the key in the ignition. Instead I stare at the bakery, *Sweet Treats*.

It's such a cute building. It's one of the only ones off of main street, but it's so close, I still get foot traffic. I put a fresh coat of pale blue paint on the cement walls and bright white on the shutters when I took over. Now the pale blue is faded and in need of a serious power wash.

Same with the shutters, only they'll have to be scrubbed by hand. The striped awning still looks decent, but the sign above it needs to be replaced.

I put everything I had into giving this bakery new life and creating a new beginning and a fresh start for myself. It's been a little over a year. I wish I hadn't. I'm exhausted, and I didn't expect running a business to be so much paperwork and marketing. All these aspects I've never considered and I'm not at all interested in. It's a money pit that sucks up every ounce of energy and minute of my time as well.

It's another mistake. That's what I'm good for. One mistake after the other.

I give myself a stern lecture as I start my car. There's no time and no place in my life for feeling sorry for myself. I'd do best to remember that. I pull out of the lot, more worked up than ever.

I wish I could just crawl into my bed and pass out, ignoring all my troubles, but I have to do this. I promised Mama I would see her everyday while she's recovering.

I sigh heavily, feeling like I'm on a knife's edge with my anxiety and lean back in my seat as I slowly stop at the red light. It's only then that I realize I've been driving without the radio on. I reach over and gently turn the volume louder so I can hear something besides my own thoughts.

My thoughts are all-encompassing, though. It's not so easy to get away from them.

I sigh. I wish I could just run away sometimes.

I should just run away. Leave this place and start over.

Guilt weighs against my chest at the thought. My car starts shuddering a bit more as it moves from the smooth asphalt to the dirt road. I blow out a breath, trying to calm myself.

There's only one thing I should be worried about, and that's getting to my parents' house on time.

Mama only asked one thing from me. Just dinner at my parents' house, every night that I'm able. Thinking of my mama makes my heart hurt that much more.

I have to stay in town and be here for her. I won't let anyone or anything get in the way of that.

Certainly not long-lost love or failing bakeries.

I pull in my parents' driveway feeling guilty for even thinking about leaving. It was a short drive and not nearly enough time to calm down.

Then again, it's a short drive practically everywhere in this town. The hardware store is about twenty minutes away, that's probably the farthest I've driven in months.

I resist the urge to scream in frustration when I look to the house across the street.

It's the Graves' house. As in Hunter Graves. I grew up across the street from Hunter.

I take a deep breath and hold it. His mother used to say we were gonna get married when we were just toddlers. She kept saying "Told ya so," when we started dating in high school.

It wasn't fair, because I believed her. She set me up.

I exhale, shaking my head.

I've barely talked to her since Hunter left. All I know is that she didn't want him to go.

I can understand that, no one wants to see their baby boy go off to war. That's not why we've barely spoken though. There's simply not much to say.

It's not her on the porch today though. It's Hunter.

And the sight of him has my thighs clenching with need.

He's a beautiful distraction. Bare-chested and looking every bit of the man I knew he'd grow up to be.

He's got a drill in his hand, and he's reaching high above his head. His corded muscles are glistening and making me forget every bad thought I ever had about him.

It looks like he's screwing something to the ceiling of the porch. My eyes finally tear away from his chiseled body and I see the porch swing sitting there.

I swallow thickly and prepare myself for a quick getaway into my parents' house. I'm not here to talk to him, and I'm not interested.

I open my car door as quietly as I can. His drill's on, and the loud hum can be heard from across the street. I shut the door as softly as I can and wince a bit when it's a tad louder than I wanted. I shouldn't even turn to see if he heard. But I do.

I take a peek over my shoulder and sure enough, his piercing green eyes are on me.

I feel caught in his gaze, my body tingling as goosebumps trail down my skin; he lowers his arm and turns to face me, his eyes never leaving mine. My heart races remembering how I caved to him last night, even if it was only for a moment.

He takes a step forward and the slight movement releases me from his hold. I walk as quickly as I can up the three wide steps to my parents' front door.

The second I'm inside, I feel like I can finally breathe. I want to turn and peek out of the peephole to see if he's still looking. But I don't.

I sag against the hard maple door and resist the urge to look, catching my breath.

It's not fair that he does this to me. I hate that he affects me so much.

This town is too small. It's so teeny-tiny that I can't escape for one moment.

"Is that you, sweetheart?"

I hear my mama call out from the kitchen and I instantly push off the door.

I'm pissed at myself for being so consumed by Hunter. I swallow thickly and right my dress, smoothing it out and pushing the loose hair out of my face.

"I'm home, Mama," I call out to her.

It's not my house. I don't live in this cute little raised ranch anymore. The one with green shutters and a porch meant for sitting out on rainy nights and watching the lightning. My house is the tiny apartment above the bakery now, but in a lot of ways, this house will always be *home*.

Mama appears in the doorway to the dining room off to my right, with a dish in one hand and a sage green kitchen towel in the other. Her dark curly locks are showing her age with a little grey at the ends near her scalp. She needs a touch-up.

"Hey Mama," I say, pushing off the door. "Need any help?"

"I can handle a few dishes." She gives me a warm smile and walks back into the kitchen.

She looks strong on the outside. She never talks about the pain either. She didn't even go into the hospital when she started having chest pains.

Some days I wonder if she would've gone in at all if my father hadn't seen her bent over holding her chest, her heart racing.

I'm glad he was there. As for my mama -- she knows better now.

That said, she's not recovering liked they'd hoped from the surgery.

I say another silent prayer that the medication for cardiovascular disease and the surgery do their job, help her recover. So far she's not getting any better, and they've done all they can do.

I inhale deeply and try to get my mind off of it.

It's going to work. I know it is. It has to.

I blink away the tears in my eyes before she can see them. She needs me to be here for her and to be strong. And I will. I made that promise to her, and I'm going to keep it.

I follow her, taking easy steps so she can't tell how much I'm hurting. I clear my throat, walking through the unlit dining room and turning on the light as I pass through.

"How's it going today?" I ask her as I lean against the large dining room doorway, peering into the kitchen.

She's standing in front of the sink, and her smile only falters slightly. She knows what I'm asking.

"Everything's fine," she says with a casual tone. *Fine*. She's not fine.

I nod and give her a weak smile. It's hard to be around her sometimes, especially when she's so relaxed about it all. She doesn't want me to worry. She wants us all to be happy, but I'm worrying. I'll worry until they tell her she's healthy again.

I turn and walk back into the dining room. I can at least be productive while I'm here. "I'll set the table for dinner."

There are stacks of mail and newspapers on the table. Growing up we never even used the table. All it did was collect lost items and mail flyers and bills. But now we use it every night.

I can faintly hear the TV in the family room as I clear off the table.

I'm sure my father's in there, passed out on the recliner. He gets up early to start his day at the factory and doesn't come home till late. I grew up with him in that old leather chair, shoved in the corner of the room. The brown coloring is worn from him sitting in it every day, watching the back of his eyelids while his shows played on the TV.

He always woke up the second you changed the channel though.

As I move the pile of newspapers to the entry table in the foyer, there's a knock at the door.

My heart stops, and I stare at it like a deer in headlights.

The knock comes again and this time it's louder.

"Can you get that?" Mama calls from the kitchen.

I lick my lips and pray it's not him. God's not listening though, cause I open the door enough for me to see Hunter. I want to slam it shut in his face.

I grip onto it and lean in as I practically hiss, "I don't have time for this."

I'm livid that he's come to my parents' house.

I try to remind myself that he doesn't know that my mama is sick. No one knows. We don't talk about it. Mama doesn't want us to. But still. There are fucking boundaries, and Hunter's pushing mine.

He rests the palm of his hand against the door, but he doesn't try to open it.

"Vi, I just wanna-"

I don't let him continue; I don't wanna hear what he has to say. Whatever it is, it's too little, too late.

"You just wanna barge back into my life and use me? Throw me away again when you've had your fill?"

My words come out in a tone even I don't recognize. I don't talk like this, to anyone, but today I've had it. I'm stressed and unhappy and I refuse to let him think I have any time for his games.

Instead of looking hurt or remorseful, Hunter looks back at me with a flash of anger.

"I didn't throw you away," he says with an even voice.

I keep his narrowed gaze and scoff at him. "I don't wanna hear it. Whatever you have to say, you can keep it to yourself."

I try to shut the door, but he holds it open. I look up at him with daggers, hating that he's stronger than me.

"What's going on?" Mama asks from behind me, and my eyes fly to hers. All the anger vanishes as my heart races.

"Who's there?" she asks as she opens the door to answer her question herself.

I watch as her forehead scrunches and her eyebrows raise.

"Hunter," she says with a bit of surprise before looking back at me. My face feels like it's on fire and I can't look her in the eyes.

"I just wanted to come on by and talk to Violet for a minute, Mrs. Shaw." Hunter's polite as he always is, but it's not gonna work this time.

"I don't think she wants to talk right now, Hunter," my mother answers.

My chest tightens with pain. My mama shouldn't be coming to my rescue. I'm a grown woman. Yet he makes me weak.

"I don't," I say with conviction, finally looking back at Hunter.

Hunter looks at me for a long moment in silence, before conceding.

He nods once and looks back at Mama. "Nice to see you again, Mrs. Shaw."

"You too, Hunter," Mama says evenly.

She leaves me in the doorway alone with him. I watch her back as she walks away, and then look to Hunter.

I expect him to say something, anything. I don't know what, but he doesn't say a damn thing.

I don't either. I have nothing else to tell him. He turns without saying goodbye to me. It hurts more than it should. It's what I wanted, I should be happy.

As I shut the door and rest my head against the wall, my heart breaks. I wish I was over him, but it's painfully obvious that I'm not.

I wish he hadn't come back here.

CHAPTER 6

HUNTER

I wander into the kitchen late the next morning to find little Abbi on the floor, trying to pour milk into a bowl of Froot Loops.

She's dressed like she's going out somewhere, in pink tights and a purple shirt. She even has her purple light-up shoes on, although they're on the wrong feet.

"Whoa, let me help," I say, taking the milk from her before she can spill it all over the place.

"Tanks Hunn." She's just now starting to say sentences and learn new words. I grin at her attempt at pronouncing my name, and fill her bowl halfway. The colorful sugary cereal swirls brightly.

"There you go," I say, grabbing a spoon out of the drawer.

She smiles at me, attacking the cereal gleefully with the spoon and her hands. The purpose of the spoon seems lost on Abbi, who mostly uses it as a shovel once the cereal is in her mouth. Milk spills down her shirt and onto the floor. I'm not used to kids or what's normal. But at least the floor and her will be easy to clean up once she's done. I lean against the counter, watching her have the time of her life, just eating.

"Oh, thank God you're up," Haley says, appearing from the basement.

She's light-haired with green eyes like me, but with about ten pounds of makeup on. She's dressed up in black pants and a long-sleeve, white blouse that's a little on the sheer side.

"Yeah, I'm supposed to go look at that lake house again," I say, going to the fridge to pour myself some orange juice. I don't know how I feel about leaving and moving out there. I want to be here for my family, but I'm sure as fuck not living at my parents' forever. The house isn't that far, but it's on the outskirts of town.

"I need you to watch Abbi," she says, putting big hoop earrings on. "I have a lunch date."

"What?" I ask with my brows furrowed.

"A lunch date," she says, making it clear that she's speaking slowly for my benefit. "Time to get back on the horse."

What the fuck? I don't mind watching Abbi, but I sure as hell have thoughts about her going out on a date. This isn't the first one either.

Abbi squeals on the floor and kicks the bowl, splashing milk everywhere. Haley looks at her with her mouth opened and then closes her eyes and sighs heavily.

She looks like she's going to snap. Shit. "I'll clean it up."

"Thanks," she says, running her hands through her hair and moving across the room to slip on a pair of heels.

I stare at her, not knowing what to say. I don't know how I feel about her going out to see other men. But I don't know if it's my place to say a damn thing about it.

I want to say something to her, but I'm not sure if I'll say the right thing. I don't want to cause tension for her or upset her. I already feel like I owe her and Abbi. I should've been there. Chris would still be alive if I hadn't fucked up.

"Mom and Dad are at the doctor, getting Dad's knee looked at. They'll be back later to help out," she says.

"Haley—"

She picks up her purse, and turns to look at me. "What?"

"Just…" I can almost see the ghost of her dead husband, haunting the space between us. "Don't you think you should slow down a little? You've gone out on two dates already since I've been home. I've barely seen you."

"*You're* telling *me* how to live my life. You were the one that brought Chris home in the first place," she says, her mouth curving down like she's tasting something bitter even though her eyes glass over. She swallows thickly and looks away.

She's hurting, and I regret bringing it up.

"Haley…" I say, setting my glass of juice on the counter.

She shifts her stance, ready to leave, and glares at me.

"Do me a favor? Watch Abbi, and stay out of my business while you do it. Can you do that?"

My voice catches in my throat. I don't like the way she's talking to me, but another part of me is fine with her anger. I deserve it. I brought those two together and then failed to bring him back home to her. This is the most we've ever talked about it. I feel useless. I don't have the words to say how I feel; I certainly don't have the ones she wants to hear. I take a deep breath, hold it for a second before letting it go.

"Yeah, alright," I say, waving her off.

She heads off, oblivious to the *bye mommy!* that Abbi lets out. I hear the click of her heels and then the door slams.

I curse beneath my breath, and turn back to Abbi. She smiles at me, milk running down her chin.

I push two pieces of bread into the toaster and think back to how they met. I brought Chris Goode home for the holiday after Haley's graduation. We'd gotten real close and he didn't have any family of his own. He and Haley hit it off right away, got engaged on his next trip home.

I couldn't be mad. Chris had a backbone of steel, but he melted whenever Haley was around. Watching them together… well, it made me hopeful for the future. Made me think of Vi, honestly.

Chris became the team leader of my SEALs unit, right after they married. Then we were shipped off to Syria, to quell the civilian violence. We did our jobs, saw plenty of bloodshed.

Hell, I personally wrought plenty of it, as the unit's designated sniper. But we got through it.

One morning it was my turn to go through routine psychological testing, care of the U.S. Navy. While I was sitting in a cramped tent and talking to the shrink about how he thought I may not be fit to continue, my squad was lighting up a tactical view point in downtown Damascus.

The operation went sideways, and an RPG ended the entire thing. Without an experienced sniper to look down over the scene, my squad had no chance. They were dead before anyone even knew what was happening.

The toast pops up, waking me from my thoughts. I grab it and eat it over the sink, keeping an eye on Abbi. I've never discussed the details of Chris' death with Haley, not once. I wasn't there. I should've kept my mouth shut to that fucking shrink. I'm fine. I'm as good as I'm gonna be, doing the shit we did. I don't know what they expect from me.

I wanted to tell her. I've wanted to tell her so many times, but she never asked.

Not even as she stood at his funeral, sobbing uncontrollably and demanding to know why God would take her husband so soon. The more emotional she got, the more distant I became.

I went back to the SEALs, went back on active duty, but my heart wasn't in it. After a couple of close calls, my new unit commander had me declared unfit.

So now I'm eating toast and watching Abbi push her cereal around with her fingers, spoon forgotten.

"Hey," I say. "What should we do this morning? Play a game? Watch TV?" I ask her to get my mind on something else.

I take her shoes off, and put them on the right way, lacing them up.

She looks thoughtful for a moment, then gleeful. "Cookie!"

She pronounces it cooo-kieee, but I understand her well enough.

"Cookie?" I ask.

"Cookie store!" she announces, throwing her arms in the air.

A piece of cereal goes flying from her hand, landing on the floor with a *plop*. I grab a paper towel and wipe off her hands before kneeling to get the cereal off the floor.

"Cookie store," I say thoughtfully. "Do you mean Sweet Treats?"

"Yeaaah!" she says, doing a happy dance in her seat. "Tweet! Tweet!"

"Alright," I say, unable to resist her charm. "Let's go to the cookie store."

I pick her up, find my keys, and head out.

Abbi is surprisingly light in my arms. She's bubbly and talkative as we walk the six blocks to the bakery. I can't understand most of what she's saying, but I let her chatter away as we go.

As far as company goes, Abbi is proving pretty good. We walk slowly, not in any hurry. I make sure to point out the buildings as we pass them.

"That's the post office," I say. "And that's the church..."

We make it to the bakery in no time and with her still smiling. The front door chimes as I open it. There's a big display case and a counter with a cash register on it, but no one is up front. It's quiet.

"Down!" Abbi says, wiggling.

I let her climb down, looking at the display. I walk over to admire the frosted cupcakes and seemingly endless cookies, crouching to see a carefully iced birthday cake. It's got huge frosting balloons all over, and it says *Happy 8th Birthday Henry!*

"Can I help you?" a soft voice comes through and makes my heart stutter.

I straighten, and look right at Violet. She stares back at me for a long second, equally surprised. She looks so damn beautiful. Her long hair is pulled back, making the soft curves of her face stand out even more.

My heart pauses as I take her in. She's got an apron wrapped around her narrow waist, making her body look extra curvy. *What the hell? Is she working here?*

"Vi," I say with a hint of confusion. "What are you doing here? Are you working for Mr. Mealey?" He's had this place all my life.

She scowls. "It's my place now."

I raise my brows. "You made all of this?"

She stares at me for a minute as if she's not sure if she even wants to answer me, and it pisses me off. She can run away, she can shut me out, but I'm not going anywhere. I want her, and I'm not gonna stop until I have her.

She spots Abbi, who has come over to cling to my leg. I can see the confusion ripple through Vi. I have the feeling that she's trying to figure out how the hell Abbi got stuck with *me*.

"Hi there," Vi says to Abbi with a much softer voice than what she gave me. She walks around the display to kneel in front of Abbi.

"Cookie Lady," Abbi says to her, and then looks to me for reassurance.

"Cookie Lady is super nice," I say. "Right, Cookie Lady?"

"Right," Vi says, looking at me uncertainly. When she turns to Abbi, though, she's all smiles. "How about you and I go around the counter and pick out a cookie?"

"Yeah!" Abbi says, grinning. "Cookie!"

Vi stands up and takes Abbi by the hand. They walk to the back of the display case, where Abbi picks out three cookies. They're huge, easily as big as my hand.

"Would you wrap up two of them, so we can take them home?" I say to Vi.

"Yeah," she says easily, not smiling at me but then giving Abbi a grin.

I look at Abbi. "I don't think your mom will be excited about you having three cookies at once, buddy."

Abbi comes around the counter, happy. She's busy eating her cookie of choice, chocolate chip and M&Ms.

I pick Abbi up and sit her down on the only bench available.

Vi smiles again, and goes to wrap up the other cookies. I pull out my wallet and toss two twenties on the counter.

"Just one," Vi says matter-of-factly, pushing the other twenty across the counter. "Cookies are only one fifty apiece."

"So keep the change," I say, shrugging.

She narrows her eyes and shakes her head, not moving to touch the other twenty as she rings up the sale.

"Okay, how about this? I talk to you for five minutes, and you keep the rest of the money as services rendered," I say, holding her gaze

Vi gives me a suspicious look, but picks up the money and puts it in the till.

"Fine. Five minutes," she says, pushing the small white bag of cookies across the counter to me and crossing her arms. She doesn't know it, but that bite in her voice and the way her breasts are pushed up only make me want her more. If she's thinking she can send me away with this cold shoulder she's given me, she's wrong. Dead fucking wrong.

"I want to say…" I clear my throat and try to think of the right words. "I want to apologize," I say, looking down at my hands. "For leaving you." I look back up and into her eyes. She's trying to hide it, but I know she's still hurting.

"What about for leaving me to the wolves?" she asks, arms crossed.

"I'm sorry, Vi."

"I told you not to call me that."

I frown as I consider her. I don't like it.

She might be upset with me, but I know I can make this right. She's my Vi. She'll always be mine. She can be mad at me for now, but that's not changing.

I take a deep breath and decide to just talk and open up to her. Maybe if I start, she'll follow my lead. And I want her to know. I want to be able to confide in her like I used to. "I feel really out of place here," I say. "Civilian life isn't what I remember it to be. But I look at you, and I think—"

The door chimes and I pause my thought; we both turn to see Mr. White, Slade's father. He looks the same as ever, a tall man in a dark suit with greying hair. He shoots me and Abbi a disdainful look, then turns to Vi. I clench my jaw.

"Good morning, Violet," he says, ignoring me. "I came in to get that tray of croissants for the bank." He walks up to the counter. "Big meeting, you know."

"Oh, of course," Vi says, darting a nervous look at me. "Let me grab it for you."

She ducks into the back, leaving me alone with Mr. White. I glance at him, but he pointedly stares at the display case.

I guess he knows who I am, then. It's a small town and we've met before, but I haven't seen him since I've been back. I haven't seen much of anyone.

Vi comes back with the tray of fresh croissants wrapped up in plastic wrap and sets it on the counter.

"Thanks for your order," she says nervously.

"Not at all, my dear. By the way, how was your date with Slade on Saturday?" Her brows shoot up, and he chuckles. "Slade keeps me in the loop on everything. I just thought I'd ask how it went."

"I, uh…" she stammers. She looks at me, blushing, and then back to Mr. White. "Good?"

"Oh good," he says, glancing at the croissants. "I think you and Slade make a nice couple. Especially considering the fact that Slade doesn't care about your *past*, apparently…"

Her past? Is that fucker referring to me?

I bite my tongue and wait for Vi to say something or give me a look so I know I can take over.

"It was just fine," she says, as though there was nothing wrong with that statement.

My hands curl into fists and I start to take a step forward, but before I can do anything about what Mr. White just said, Abbi announces that she's done eating.

"All done!" she says, waving her sticky, chocolate-covered hands at me. "Allllll done."

Thank fuck she reminded me she was here. I'm on edge with anger and doing my best to contain it. I look back at Mr. White and see him for the man he's always been. If Abbi wasn't here, I'd slam my fist into his jaw.

I look back at Vi and she's not showing any concern.

I huff out a breath and walk over to pick Abbi up. It's definitely time for us to go. I turn toward the door.

"Wait!" Vi calls as I get to the front door.

I turn back, and she's holding the white paper bag with my extra cookies in it. "Don't forget these."

I trudge over and take them from her, not making eye contact. I'm pissed, and if I'm not careful, my anger will splash over onto Vi.

I'm pushing my way out with Abbi in my arms when I hear Vi's parting words.

"See you later?" she says as though it's a question.

It might be in my imagination, but I think it sounds hopeful. I straighten up and look back at her. She's not pissed, and she's asking to see me again.

"For that five minutes I owe you," she tacks on quickly. I look past her and see Mr. White looking pissed as hell.

I give her a small grin. "I'll swing by again."

CHAPTER 7

VIOLET

I've never felt so uncomfortable in my entire life. My cheeks burn, and the back of my neck feels like it's on fire.

I can't imagine Mr. White didn't know exactly what he was doing bringing up the fact that I was on a date with Slade in front of Hunter. I wish he'd just leave. I'm not even really listening to him.

I just want to know what Hunter was going to say. I shouldn't be hanging on to every word coming out of his gorgeous mouth, but I am. I'm ashamed that I seem to be falling for his charm again, but I can't help it.

When I look at him, I see the boy I fell in love with and the way he says my name … it all comes back to me.

I giggled at him as he took my hand in his and led me through the back path of the woods to the creek. It was

64

our favorite place to hide away and get lost in each other's kisses and innocent touches.

We'd been together almost three months and it finally felt like... like it was real. Like it wasn't going to end any minute now.

A wide smile made his handsome face even more attractive as he ducked under the thick branch of a tree.

I lowered my head and kept up, walking as fast as I could across the uneven dirt floor littered with sticks and random stones.

"Why are you in such a rush tonight?" I asked him with humor as he pulled on my hand.

He looked back at me, moving the branches out of my way.

"You'll see, Vi."

His face was so happy, and my heart seemed to melt.

It was the first time he called me Vi. The tone of his voice was so easy and full of warmth. It was as if in that moment, I was his. His Vi.

"Come on," he said, tugging once again. I hadn't realized I'd stopped.

He led me through the opening to a small clearing by the creek and I looked all around for whatever it was he was anxious to see.

He wrapped his arms around my waist and pulled my back into his hard chest. I remember his hot breath on my neck sending goose-bumps down my arms as he lowered his head and whispered into my ear.

"Look up."

I did in an instant, letting my head rest against his broad shoulder.

Above us were so many bright white stars, lighting up the dark night. Shooting stars. My eyes widened, and my lips parted. It was so beautiful. The sky was littered with bright lights and streaks of wonder.

"It's the aurora borealis," he said quietly. I wrapped my arms on top of his, loving how his body warmed me in the chill of the night. "I thought you'd like it."

I kept my eyes focused on the stars, but I was mesmerized by the sincerity in his voice and the comfort of his touch. "I love it."

*M*r. White clears his throat, snapping me out of the sweet memory and back to this bullshit reality. Time has changed everything.

I can't look at him as the front door closes and Hunter walks out with his little niece in his arms.

I feel so guilty. I don't even know what for! I'm not seeing either Hunter or Slade.

I turn around and start cleaning the marble cutting board. There's a bit of icing on it left over from the cookies that needs to be scraped off before it hardens.

"Can I get you anything else while you're in here?" I ask.

I don't turn around. I'm focused on the mess I've made, and just trying to clean it up. I feel like I've had enough of Mr. White and enough of these games.

I need him though. I need that fucking loan. I have too much credit card debt and I've been denied so many times it's not funny. He's my last hope. I fucking hate it.

"You know it doesn't look good on my family name for you

to be talking to that young man," Mr. White says, in a lowered voice that forces me to turn around and stare him down.

"I'm sorry?"

I give him a look that lets him know I'm pissed off. I may feel bad about how everything's progressing, and the fact that I'm just not into Slade like I probably should be.

But I am not going to let him accuse me of anything. Or talk down about Hunter.

"Slade's a good man, isn't he?" he asks me.

I grab the small towel on the counter and wipe down my hands. My brows are pinched and no matter how hard I try, I can't soften them. My breath is caught in my chest. I feel stuck.

"He is," I answer simply.

There's certainly nothing wrong with him. Even if there was, I'm not going to be rude.

"He deserves a good woman." My skin prickles with insecurity as I stare back at Mr. White. "I understand you and Mr. Graves had a little thing going on a few years ago, but Slade assured me that it was just a mistake."

My heart hammers in my chest. How the hell did I fall into this conversation? It's been years since anyone has had the nerve to bring that up to me. Let alone a grown man.

"I fail to see what you're getting at, Mr. White," I say. I keep a straight face, daring him to accuse me of something, or anything or whatever the hell he's getting at. My hands feel numb and I'm sick to my stomach, but I refuse to back down.

"I just want to make sure we're on the same page, Miss Shaw."

"And what page is that?" I ask in an even voice that makes me feel proud.

Inside I'm breaking down, but at least I look calm and strong on the surface.

"That the loan you need isn't supported by the money the business is bringing in."

My lips turn down instantly into a pathetic frown and my heart stops beating. Tears threaten to prick my eyes, but I hold them back.

Fuck him. I won't let him see me cry.

He looks down and picks at his fingernail before looking back at me.

"Of course, I always make an exception for the people my son is fond of."

I feel numb. I don't know how to respond.

"I'm sure we'll work something out," he says, smiling that creepy smile. "Anyway…"

He takes the tray of croissants, and leaves the store. The door chimes on his way out.

Although I'm looking at the counter, trying to hold back everything threatening to come up, I swear I see his eyes roaming my body.

I've never felt so violated in my life. I don't know what to do or say. I feel weak and helpless, but more than that, I'm angry.

I can't stand the men in this damn town. They can all go
screw themselves.

CHAPTER 8

HUNTER

I slide a hand over the fender of the souped-up, cherry red '67 Corvette. The metal's cold and smooth and feels just right. A small grin plays at my lips. I can't help it. Cars were my one pleasure back on base. Jared just pulled the dusty cover off it, showing me the car as it stands in his garage.

"Man, this is a sexy hunk of steel," I say.

Jared nods, drinking from his can of Miller Lite. "Yeah. My dad and I finished the outside, but not the inside."

"You mean you can't start it?" I say, admiring the hand-tooled leather seats.

"Yeah. You know, Dad passed away two years ago, but we stopped working on the car about five years ago."

"Mind if I pop the hood?" I ask, looking at Jared. "I picked up a thing or two in the Navy, working in the mechanic's shop. I did that for my first two years, on my downtime during BUD/S training."

"Sure, sure," Jared says, waving a hand. "Go ahead, Mr. Navy SEAL."

I smirk at him and open the driver's side door to pop the hood. When I get a look at the engine, I see that the distributor is badly damaged, the alternator's busted and in need of replacement, and everything needs a good dusting.

"I think this is fixable, if you can find the parts," I tell Jared.

"Really?" he says, looking surprised.

"Yeah. I mean, you'll probably have to order parts online, and they might be a couple grand, because the car's so old... but we could get it running."

"No shit," he says, shaking his head in disbelief. "I just kept it because it seemed like a waste to throw it away. Little did I know, my best friend went to war and came back a mechanic. You should open a shop, man."

I glance at him, expecting him to be teasing, but he's serious. I brush off my hands and close the hood. He adds, "We could use a good one."

"I don't know," I say and shrug. "I do have to do something..."

"Knock knock!" says Krissy, Jared's wife. She's way more beautiful than Jared, slim and platinum blonde. He's a lucky bastard. "I just came out to see if you were staying for dinner, Hunter."

"I can't," I say, shaking my head. "Thanks, though."

"Well, dinner's almost ready," she says, looking pointedly at Jared. "Nice to see you, Hunter."

She leaves with a swish, making me smile.

Vi would get along with her, I think to myself. Jared started seeing Krissy right before I ended things with Vi. I look down and wipe my hands on my jeans. The memory makes me tense.

"Alright, I'm gonna walk home," I say, bumping Jared on the shoulder. "See you later."

Jared smiles. "See you."

I head outside into the early evening air. I can feel the hint of fall in the air, almost cold. I start walking, intending to make it home, but I keep thinking about Violet.

Mostly about her parting words about seeing her later.

I could swing by now, but she's probably closed. I didn't specify her shop though, maybe I could swing by her house. Something tells me that wouldn't go over as well though. Like the last time I stopped by.

I stand in front of my parents' house and look over to hers. She didn't want to see me the other day, but I *told* her I'd swing by. I cluck my tongue and wonder if I'll be pushing my luck or not. Fuck, I've always been pushing my luck with Vi. That thought gets my legs moving. I look both ways and jog across the narrow street and onto their gravel driveway.

She may not wanna talk right now, but she did the other day. And I sure as hell wanna talk to her.

I jog up the three stairs and hold my fist up to the door.

I stand there for a second, then blow out a breath.

Vi belongs with me, not with that asshole Slade, and not anyone else. She's mine. I'm more sure of it than I've ever been of anything in my life.

I'll do whatever I have to do to get her back. I know she wants me, I just have to win her over.

I knock three times, heart beating hard in my chest. I hear someone coming to the door, but the footsteps don't sound like Vi, it's more of a shuffle than anything else.

When the door opens, it's Mrs. Shaw, Violet's mother. She's wrapped in so many layers of shawls, she looks like she's gotta be burning up. She blinks at me from behind oversized glasses. The years haven't been kind to her. I wasn't expecting her to answer. It takes me aback, and my confidence is ripped out from under me.

"Hunter," she says suspiciously. "I didn't expect to see you here."

"Sorry, Mrs. Shaw. I was hoping to find Vi." I feel like I did five years ago, almost six. The first time I came up these steps to ask Vi on a date. My palms were sweaty and I was nervous as hell. Her father answered then. At least it's not him at the door now.

Her eyebrows lift. "She lives down the street, above her bakery."

"Ah. Well... thanks," I say.

"You know it's not a nice thing to come back here and try to get between two people," Mrs. Shaw says as I turn my shoulder to walk away.

I turn slowly back to her and look her in the eyes as I say, "I'm not sure what you mean. There's no two people to get between." I know what she's getting at, but I'd rather her be upfront with it. Everyone in this town likes to skirt around issues. I'm more of a head-on kinda guy. "If you're talking about Violet and Slade, you're mistaken. As far as I know, they aren't a couple."

She frowns at me, but holds my gaze as her eyes narrow. "I always liked you, Hunter. You were good people, your whole family is. But what you did hurt my baby girl."

It's hard looking her in her eyes as they glaze over with tears. Fuck, it reminds me of the day I broke Vi's heart. I take it though. I'm gonna have to make it up to both of them then, and I will. I open my mouth to apologize, but she goes in for another kill shot.

"I liked you more than I ever liked Slade, but at least he has good intentions, marriage intentions." That pisses me off. It takes a lot of restraint not to show it.

"Slade's not gonna marry your daughter. And if he did, she wouldn't be happy." The thought of her with a ring on her finger other than one I give her makes adrenaline spike in my blood. "What good is a marriage if Vi's going to spend the whole time belittled and with someone she doesn't want to be with?"

"She can be with whoever she wants-"

"Well, she doesn't want Slade, and I'm going to make damn sure she wants me. I'll make it up to her, and I'll make sure she's happy." I turn to walk down the steps, but I add, looking over my shoulder, "I'll make damn sure I do right by her."

CHAPTER 9

VIOLET

*T*he gravel of my parents' driveway crunches beneath my feet as I get out of my car. I heft the grocery bags, full of the supplies to make a sheet cake. I spot my mama on the front porch, sitting in a rocking chair beneath a pile of blankets.

"Hey," I say, stopping when I'm in front of her. "I brought by some day-old bread for your bird feeders."

"Well, sit down for a minute, won't you?" my mama says, pulling up the blankets around her chest.

"Sure," I answer, sitting down on the chair and setting my bags down. I run my fingers over the worn cushion beside me. "Are you cold?"

"One of the many blessings of poor circulation," my mama jokes. "But enough about me. I want to hear about you. How are things at the bakery?"

"Good," I say, dropping my eyes and picking at a thread on the cushion. "You know."

"You said something on the phone yesterday about one of the ovens not working," she says, frowning.

"Yeah. It's a little hard to keep up with the school's catering orders without the second oven," I admit. "It's okay, though. I've been bringing some of the orders home upstairs and doing them there. It's not too bad, but there's not much space."

"Oh, are you going to do some baking here, then?"

I bite my lip. "If that's okay with you. The oven being broken is just temporary, I'm sure."

I'm not completely honest with her, but I think if she was in my position, she'd do the same.

"Of course," she says, waving toward the house. "It's your home too, you know."

"Thanks," I say, sighing. "I have to make a sheet cake for the elementary school today, or I could lose their contract."

Something passes between us, a note of understanding.

"Do you need money?" she asks, her bright blue eyes shrewd.

"Oh, Mama... I can't accept charity from you," I say with a sigh. "You and Dad put me through college, and I hardly use the degree I got. I guess I really thought I'd get out of school and be able to get a teaching position easy."

"If you'd moved to the city, maybe," my mama says, closing her eyes and leaning her head against her chair.

I feel guilty. My mama and dad spent nearly everything they had to put me through school, refusing to take a cent from me. Then my mama got sick, and I just know hospital bills are mounting, forming a colossal pile somewhere inside the house.

I wish I could help, but I'm not doing any better than they are.

"Yeah, maybe so," I muse, in answer to my mama's statement. "Anyway, that's life. What is it they say? 'We plan, God laughs.'"

My mama opens her eyes and smiles.

"That's right. I meant to ask, how are things with you and Slade?"

I wrinkle my nose. "Okay."

She chuckles. "Just okay?"

"Yeah. Just... okay. I don't know."

My mama pushes the blankets off of one arm and puts her hand in mine. I'm surprised at how cool her hand is, like she hasn't been under the pile of blankets for an hour.

"Don't worry, sweetheart," she says, giving my hand a squeeze. "You'll find the man of your dreams. You never know, you may have already met him."

My eyes fill with tears at the sage advice she's giving me. I squeeze her hand in return, then clear my throat.

"I should go inside and start baking," I say, rising from the chair.

"Okay, honey."

I kiss her on the top of her head as she buries herself in blankets again.

"I'll bring you a spoonful of frosting," I promise.

"Mmmhmm," she says, closing her eyes again. "My favorite."

I blow out a breath as I pick up my grocery bags and head inside. I unpack the baking supplies, thinking about what my mama said.

You may have already met him, she said.

That makes me think of Hunter, of his smile and his strong arms. Try as I might, I can't think of anyone else.

I sigh and push the thought away, focusing on my cake batter.

CHAPTER 10

HUNTER

I hate waiting to talk to Vi. I've been by her place at the bakery twice now, and she wasn't there either time. Last night I waited there for hours. She never showed, and I was pissed. If I'm honest with myself, I was worried, too.

She had to have been staying somewhere else and the thought that she was with Slade is a real possibility. When I finally dragged my ass back home, I saw her car in her parents' driveway. I almost stormed over there, but I stopped myself, thinking I should wait till it wasn't the middle of the night and I wasn't making an ass of myself, acting on jealousy.

This morning she wasn't there and she wasn't at the bakery either. The note said she was doing deliveries. I've been gone for years, and now that I'm back I can't get one fucking minute with her. Figures.

My pops drops the wrench on the floor of the garage with a

loud bang, startling me from my thoughts. He's digging through his old toolbox taking an inventory of what he's got.

"Careful, old man," I joke with him. He looks up at me with a raised brow before bending over with a loud sigh and picking it up.

"Careful yourself, son," he says as he sets the wrench down on the steel bench.

"So what'd ya think?" I walk over to him and lean against the steel counter, looking at the old junk of a VW buggy in the garage. It was supposed to be my sister's car, but we never got around to fixing it. I brace my hands on the bench and look over to him as I say, "I could be a mechanic, I think." Ever since Jared planted the seed, the idea has been growing and giving me an outlet to focus on. I think I'd fucking love it.

"Sure you could," he says, but he doesn't look me in the eyes as he adds, "It'll cost a pretty penny to get it up and running though."

I nod my head; I know it will, but I've got the cash flow to get it started. I never really spent a dime in the Navy. I didn't have to. So I've got enough to get it started. I've already looked into it. I've got more than enough.

"I'm not sure the bank is gonna go out on a limb for you without you having any income right now, but-"

I cut my pops off right there. "I don't need the Whites' money for this." My voice is louder than it should be. I look past him and stare at the tools hanging from the pegboard on the back wall. "It's not a matter of getting money."

My words still come out a little harsher than I mean for them to. I push off the bench and stalk to the buggy to calm my ass down. Pops doesn't need my anger. No one does. I just don't like seeing Slade's hands on my girl. I don't like the way his father talked to her either. Vi doesn't deserve that, she's better than both of them. The Whites can go fuck themselves.

"Something wrong with the Whites?" Pops asks me as he closes the toolbox and leans against the buggy, eyeing me like he doesn't know what's going on.

"I don't care for either of them, Slade or his father, to be honest." I turn my head to look him in the eyes. "I don't like Slade and Violet together."

"You're wound up over a girl you have no claim to." It pisses me off that he has the balls to say that, but then he keeps going, "And to make matters worse, you're giving that girl a bad name."

I temper my anger slightly as I ask, "Oh yeah, how's that?"

"That she's fooling around with you again." He shakes his head and says, "She doesn't need that, Hunter. You gotta let it go."

"I'm not letting it go. I'm not losing her again."

He looks exasperated. "It's not losing when you haven't got anything to lose!"

My voice is hard and I hold his angry gaze. "She's mine. She's always been mine, and she'll always be mine."

"Don't be stupid, Hunter," he scoffs at me, pissing me off. "She's moved on, and you need to lay that puppy dog love to bed where it belongs."

I push off the car and take a step closer to my father. I've never been so fucking angry at this man. I've always looked up to him. Always taken his advice. But right now, all I wanna do is beat the shit out of him. "I never should've let her go."

"Is that the son I raised?" He kicks off the car and meets me chest to chest as he adds, "A selfish prick who'd make a woman wait on him?"

"It was her choice." I keep my ground. "She wanted to wait on me coming home. If she wanted that, I should've given her that. 'Cause I wanted it, too."

He huffs a humorless laugh and walks around me. "You're being a damn fool, Hunter."

"I was a fool to listen to you." I bite out my words, my hands balling into fists. I mean it, too. What we had was real, and it was worth fighting for.

He flinches at my words, and the hard lines on his face slip for a moment. "Do what you want, Hunter." His voice is lowered and full of disappointment. "All you're doing is hurting that poor girl." With that he opens the garage door and lets it close silently behind him as he goes back inside.

My chest heaves with anger, and I take a minute to calm myself down. I feel like everyone's rooting against us, but I don't give a fuck.

She's mine.

I don't care where she is. This town is small; I'll find her. I'm not going to leave her alone until I make it damn clear that I want her back. I just need one chance. Just one.

CHAPTER 11

VIOLET

I heft the trays of cookies for the elementary school Fall Ball, hitching them up on my hip as I walk into the school. I smile at the macaroni art self-portraits and finger-painted families hanging on the wall just inside the double doors.

I stop to admire the trophies in their display case, and the pictures of grinning teams of children beside them. My picture used to be up there. The memory makes me smile some. It feels good here. I can hear sneakers squeaking across the gym floor, the double doors are open a few classrooms up.

I look down at the cookies I'm holding, wondering why I'm baking for a living. How much of what I do is just because Mr. Mealey gave me an opportunity to buy the bakery? I was substitute teaching when I came home. I needed to find a job quick, and working a day or two a week, just wasn't cutting it. Teacher positions are slim in this job market.

I always dreamed of having a classroom and students of my

own, but that's all it is. A dream. Now I'm living a different life.

I sigh and move down the hallway, the trays still balanced on my hip. I see a group of students in the gym as I pass, playing some game. Another group of students is going down the hall, all following their teacher like ducklings.

"Cookie!"

I turn my head to see Abbi hurrying toward me, Krissy following her. Krissy and I knew each other well in high school, but now we're just acquaintances.

Krissy looks elegant, her red wrap dress fitting her thin frame well. I know she married Jared. I remember how jealous I was. I could've had that with Hunter. I felt like a horrible human being for being upset with someone else's happiness. But it was all I could think when I saw their picture in the paper. They're practically the town sweethearts.

She catches Abbi just a few feet from me, and scoops her up, making Abbi cry out with a squeal.

"Hey Violet," Krissy says, exasperated. "Sorry."

"No, it's fine," I say, moving closer to say hi to Abbi. "Abbi comes into my shop a lot to get cookies."

"Cookie! Cookie!" Abbi insists, tears starting to take over her voice.

"I'm in charge of the daycare today," Krissy says, rolling her eyes. "Miss Abigail was supposed to go home an hour ago, but her mom is MIA. I had to call her uncle. Didn't I, Abbi?"

"Hunter?" I say.

"Yep. So he should be here in a minute," Krissy says to Abbi. "It's okay, buddy. It's okay."

Abbi is throwing a temper tantrum, but Krissy's unflappable.

"Haley is MIA? No idea where she is?" I ask, shifting the trays to my other hip.

"No," Krissy said, shaking her head. "Apparently not."

I frown. I heard that Haley's husband died while in service to the Navy, and I remember how torn up about it she was. She was crying all the time: in the produce section of grocery store, at red lights, in church. My heart went out to her. It still does. I can't even imagine it. She seems to be dealing with the grief differently now. If the rumor mills are anything to go by, she's been getting over Chris, by getting under other men. I try to stay out of those conversations. I try not to judge. But it makes my heart hurt for her even more.

What I remember most was that when Chris passed away, is that I kept thinking, *what if it had been Hunter?* I couldn't sleep, especially when I knew they worked together. I try to shake the thoughts as my throat closes with sadness.

"I'm here," a masculine voice sounds down the hallway.

I turn around, and there's Hunter, striding down the hallway. I bite my lip and give him a once-over, looking at his black Nine Inch Nails tee shirt and dark jeans. More specifically, looking at his muscular arms, at the stomach I know is flat and hard beneath that shirt.

He sees me with Krissy and Abbi, and his brow knits.

"I have to go," I say to Krissy, ripping my eyes from Hunter.

"Sure. See you around," she says, moving away from me

85

toward Hunter. I turn and halfway run down the hall, at least as well as I can with the trays of cookies in my hands.

"Vi!" Hunter calls, but I'm already turning the corner.

I hear the rumble of his voice as he says something to Krissy, but I surge ahead. I don't have time for him. I don't have time for anything but the task at hand, and running errands like this one.

Mrs. Pine is waiting for me when I finally get to the cafeteria. I drop the cookies off in a hurry, and get the hell out of there as fast as I can.

I purposely exit the building, taking the long way around to get to my car. Better that I don't run into *him*.

But when I get back to my car, he's leaning against the door, looking smug. I slow as I approach the car, blowing out a breath.

"Where's Abbi?" I ask.

"Playing a video game in my truck."

He points to the truck parked two spaces over from mine. The window's down and I can hear the high-pitched noises from whatever she's playing. I bite my lip, feeling suddenly shy. My heart starts pounding just being this close to him.

"Oh. Well..." I say, stopping a foot from Hunter. "Do you think you could move?"

"That depends. Will you go out with me tonight?" he asks, cocking a brow.

"I... I can't," I say, shaking my head.

"Why?" he asks, pushing himself off my car.

"I have to… um… do stuff," I say lamely.

"Stuff?" he asks, moving closer, until he's just an inch away.

I could move back. I could slap him, for getting too close. But I don't do either.

Instead I let my head fall back, looking up at him. I lick my lips, trying not to think of the taste of him, trying to ignore how my body ignites with desire.

"Bakery stuff," I say. "Baking. I have to make a cake." I swallow thickly and try to remember if I really do need to bake something.

I'm aware that I sound like an idiot. His hand comes out to brush back a strand of my hair and tuck it behind my ear.

I don't want to, but I lean into his touch. His hand opens and cups the back of my head. I look up into those emerald green eyes, as hypnotic now as they were the first day I saw him.

He leans down and brushes his lips over mine, a burning brand. I curl my hand in his hair and kiss him harder, his blatant sensuality catching like tinder.

I press my lips to his, so lush and firm. I open my mouth almost against my will, needing to taste him. He takes over the kiss, his tongue stroking mine in long, firm sweeps.

I groan. Nothing has ever felt so good as I feel right now, I swear it. His touch feels so calming, so right, just like he used to, like he never left me.

He breaks the kiss abruptly, leaning his forehead against mine. He's breathing a little harshly; now that I think about it, I am, too.

We stand like that for a few seconds, just breathing each other in.

"Seven p.m. tonight," he says, releasing me and stepping back.

I bring my fingers to my lips, feeling somehow bereft. I nod, feeling completely out of it.

Hunter grins again, that cocky expression still on his face. Then he winks at me, before heading to his truck. I stand there like a fool, watching him pull out of the parking lot.

I finally manage to get in my car, still adrift and lean my head back, letting out a slow exhale.

I have a date tonight. A date with Hunter.

I don't even know how to feel. I start my car and pull out of the parking lot, mulling everything over.

CHAPTER 12

I take a look in the rearview mirror, feeling like I need to get more control on this situation. I'm sweating; I'm so damn nervous.

She makes me nervous.

I need tonight to go right. I've got everything planned out. If Vi's anything like I remember, she's going to love every minute of it.

I park the car in front of the bakery. It's late and the bakery is closed, but the light above the storefront is on. The yellow glow from the window of her apartment spills into the night.

I'm not sure what I should do. If I should walk up to the bakery door and knock, or call her. Or maybe she's got a door around back for her apartment; I'm not sure. She doesn't give me a minute to figure it out though. She pulls the thin curtain back and I can easily make out her silhouette.

It's showtime. I get out of the truck and make my way up the paved parking lot with my hands in my pocket. I take slow steps and stop a few feet in front of my truck.

My heart's beating fast, waiting for Vi. When she finally steps out into the faint light from my truck, it nearly stops. She's so fucking beautiful.

Her long, dark hair spills over her shoulders and just past her breasts. Her cream blouse is unbuttoned, just at the top, so I can make out the soft curves of her figure. Her worn jeans hug every inch of her as she walks to me with a shyness she hasn't showed me in a long time.

"Vi," I say as I take a step closer to her.

She stops in her path and grips her clutch in both hands.

"Hunter," she says with that softness in her voice that I remember from years ago.

It feels like everything clicks into place. I've got a piece of her right now. A piece of our past that she's not denying.

I walk around to the passenger door and open it for her.

"Where are we going?" she asks.

She doesn't make a move to get in. I can tell she's still walking a knife's edge with whether or not to trust me, but I'll show her she can. I'll prove to her I'm still the man she once loved. I can be that man again. For her.

"A late-night picnic on the hill." It's where I used to take her. I'm hoping it gets me some brownie points.

A soft smile plays at her lips, and a beautiful blush rises to her cheeks. "You don't play fair, Hunter Graves."

I let a rough chuckle vibrate through my chest and hold her hand as she steps into the truck. She looks so small in it.

I carefully shut the door and jog around the front of the truck to get in. As if waiting too long to start driving will give her another chance to run.

When I get in, she turns up the radio and sits back in her seat, letting out a small yawn. Her hand covers her face, and she looks away with a smile when she feels my eyes on her. The sight of her like this, at ease with me, is everything I've wanted. I feel whole again.

A small bit of guilt weighs down on me for even thinking I can be whole. Chris is still gone because of me. My sister will never have a second chance. He's gone, and there's nothing she can do about it. She can't go back like I'm trying to do.

"You okay?" Vi's voice is laced with concern.

I put the truck into reverse and try to get my mind back on the present. The guilt is still pushing hard on my chest, but I ignore it. Part of me wants to open up to her, but I want this date to be perfect. I want to win her back.

"Yeah," I say absently, paying attention to the road.

My heart's beating faster, and I'm trying to push down the anxiety I'm feeling.

"You're different." I hear Vi's soft words, and I turn to look at her.

Yeah, I am different. In a lot of ways.

I swallow the lump in my throat and nod.

"Yeah, I am." I look back to the road and then settle a hand on her thigh, rubbing my thumb back and forth against her jeans. "I'm still the man you fell in love with though."

She flinches at my words, and I wish I could take them back.

Her body tenses and she looks out the window, shoving her thumb in her mouth to bite on her nail.

"I'm sorry I hurt you." I take my time driving up to the hill and put it all out there. "I know I did. I know I can't take it back, but if you'll let me, I'll make it right."

She looks at me with sad blue eyes. "You can't make it right, Hunter."

I squeeze her thigh as the truck rocks with the uneven road.

"Just give me a chance, Vi."

"I am." She puts her hand over mine, and it soothes some of my worry and closes a bit of the distance between us. "That's what this is."

I nod, giving her leg another short squeeze and park the car as close to the clearing as I can.

She gives me a small smile.

"Are we gonna see shooting stars?" Her voice is so small, and a little sad.

"I don't think so, not tonight," I say. I know what she's talking about, and I wish I could give her what she wants. If I could make it happen, I would. But some things, I can't control.

Her eyes fall to the ground. I move my hand on top of hers and wait for her to look back at me. "There are more nights, Vi. We'll come back."

Her soft blue eyes reach mine and I lean in, planting a small kiss on her lips. She molds her lips to mine and I pull back, cupping her face in my hand. I look down at her, and her eyes are still closed. It reminds me of the first time I ever kissed her.

Hope blooms in my chest as I fall back into my seat and open the door.

For the first time since I've come home, I feel like I've got a real chance with her. I feel like she's not fighting me. But our past is still keeping us apart.

I open her door and help her down, and she lets me, placing her small hand in mine easily.

I reach behind the passenger seat for the big ass picnic basket with the blanket in it and our packed dinner. I let Haley help me pick what to get, but I made sure to get Vi's favorite dessert, black raspberry crumb cake. I would've grabbed sunflowers too if they'd had them at the florist. No luck though.

"I hope you're hungry," I say to her, closing the door and taking her hand.

She smiles, but doesn't answer. There's a little tension that's still between us. It doesn't help that I'm not right in the head and she doesn't know why. We make our way through the woods with her hand in mine, holding me tightly.

"You're cheating," she says playfully.

It makes me grin at her and my heartbeat picks up faster. If I wasn't cheating, I wouldn't be trying.

I move a thick branch out of the way for her to duck under and kick some of the smaller sticks off the path. Damn kids around here must not know about this place, seeing as how the path's covered with other growth. We always came here. It's the best place there is to get away from town while still being here.

"I know," I answer her with a smile that makes her laugh. "I can use all the help I can get."

Her brows raise, and she clears her throat. I prepare myself for some snappy comment, but she keeps walking ahead and keeps her mouth shut.

Part of me's grateful for that. But I want my Vi back, and if that means she's gotta let me have it, I'd rather her beat the shit out of me than hide her pain and just play along.

She knows right where to go, leading the way rather than waiting on me and I follow her the last few steps to the clearing in silence.

The stars are clear and bright above us. There aren't many, but the sky is bright. There's no need for the lanterns I packed. But I pull them out anyway. As I set the basket down I look up at her. The light gives her a youthful glow. She's staring at the sky with a look of wonder.

"I haven't been here since you left," she says in a soft voice as I lay the blanket out.

The blanket brushes her calf before settling to the ground. She takes a deep breath and crouches to the ground before sitting on it and letting out an easy sigh.

"I thought about this place all the time while I was away."

"You did?" she asks.

"Almost every night."

This place was always on my mind when I was writing to her. The letters that I wrote, but never sent. I brought them tonight. My heart beats a little faster, and my palms turn sweaty. I'm not sure I want to show her. A part of me feels

94

like a coward for even writing them. I should've sent them to her, or never written a damn thing.

Before I can convince myself not to give them to her, I lay it all out. The only thing I have worth losing is her, and if there's any chance that the letters can help me win her over, I'm going to take it.

"I wrote to you," I say, pulling out the sandwiches. The letters are underneath them. I lay one in front of her as she eyes me with caution.

"I never got a letter." I can feel her eyes on me, so I look up and see the hurt on her face. "Not a single one."

I'm such a fucking bastard.

I clear my throat and add, "I didn't send them."

I pull the bundle of them out and slide them over the blanket to her. There are over two hundred of them, neatly stacked and tied with twine. I only stopped writing after Chris was killed. I couldn't anymore.

I couldn't get the words out right. I couldn't tell her. I couldn't tell anyone.

"Why?" she asks with a bite of exasperation.

Maybe I should've waited.

"'Cause I never wanted it to end with you. I fucking loved you, Vi. You were my world." All I can hear is the blood rushing in my ears. It's silent for a moment. The tips of her fingers run along the twine, but she doesn't pick up the letters.

"Then why do it?" she asks. "Why break my heart if you

really wanted to be with me?" she asks, and her voice takes on a hard edge. Her anger is coming through.

"I thought it was the right thing to do. To not keep you waiting on me, knowing I might never come back." *Like Chris.* Vi starts shaking her head with her lips parted, and her hands balled into fists. She's gearing up for a fight.

I push the letters and the basket out of the way and pull her small body close to me.

"Vi, I was wrong. I was dead fucking wrong to let you go." Her jaw is clenched, and she's hardly looking at me. "I know that now, and I'm sorry. I'm an asshole for doing it. I'm a dumb fucker who doesn't deserve you. But I want you. I want what we had back then." Her eyes look up at me through her thick lashes, glassy with tears, but she's silent. "Just tell me what to do."

I lean down, resting my forehead against hers. She's quiet.

"I'll do anything, I promise."

She tilts her head and kisses me right then. A soft, sweet kiss. Molding her lips to mine.

I try to deepen it, but she pulls back, breaking it, and I hate it.

I want more. I want *her.*

I keep my eyes closed and whisper.

"Forgive me, Vi."

She pushes her lips against mine in a chaste kiss. "I'm trying."

I smile against her lips. At least she's being honest with me. Her tense body softens in my arms, and I hold her closer to me. She feels so warm compared to the chill of the night.

In that moment I realize how close we are with her in my lap. My hand splays along her back. I wrap my arms tighter around her, and feel her breasts against my chest.

"I never stopped loving you," I whisper.

My lips gently brush against the shell of her ear. I leave a trail of open-mouthed kisses down her neck and to the small dip in her throat.

A soft moan escapes her lips as I lay her down on the blanket. My forearm hits the basket, and I shove it away.

"I want you, Vi," I whisper into the crook of her neck.

Her skin is so soft and warm. I push my body on top of hers, caging her in and getting lost in the memory of her body writhing under mine. My dick hardens with need. I *need* her. I need to make it right and show her that I love her. To hear her soft moans, to feel her small warm body trembling beneath me.

"I'm sorry, Hunter."

I pull back slightly at Vi's words, snapping out of the lust-filled haze clouding my head.

"I can't do this," she says, pushing her hands against my chest.

She's shaking her head and pushing me off of her. I brace my hand on the grass and let her up. What the fuck happened?

"Vi?" I slowly rise as she stands and looks at me like I hurt her. "Vi, you okay?"

"No, Hunter. I'm not okay. The last time you said those words to me, you ruined me. You hurt me more than anyone ever has, and... I don't trust you." Her words hurt, but worse than that, it's seeing the genuine pain on her face.

97

"I don't trust anyone," she says and her voice cracks. "I'm afraid to let anyone in. And it's all because of you."

She can barely get the words out. Her eyes are red and glassy.

Damn, what'd I do? I raise my hands as though she's a wounded animal. This is good. She's getting it out. *Get it all out, Vi.*

I wait for her to say something else. For her to scream at me, pound her fists against my chest, whatever she wants to do, but instead she looks over her shoulder.

"Vi, don't leave." As soon as I say the words, she turns to bolt. I quickly catch up to her and wrap her in my arms.

"Get off of me, Hunter!" she says weakly, pushing against me as she heaves in a sob.

"Just a minute. Just calm down and if you wanna leave, you can go." I kiss her hair as she stops trying to shove me away. I don't wanna let her go, I don't want her to run from me anymore. "Just try to calm down, Vi. It's alright."

She shakes her head against my chest and then lays her cheek flat against me. She's not fighting me anymore, but she's not okay either.

"It's not alright, Hunter. It's not gonna be alright... I don't want you."

Her words slam against me like a punch to the gut. My hold on her loosens as my heart falls in my chest. She backs away slowly, moving the hair from her face. Her cheeks are reddened and tearstained.

"I loved you once, but I can't anymore." She holds my gaze as she takes a step back.

"Let me drive you home," I say in an even voice I don't recognize. As if this conversation didn't happen. Not to me. Not to us.

Her words echo in my head. *She doesn't want me*. But I want to deny it.

"No," she says, shaking her head. "I want to go home. Alone. I just wanna be alone."

With that, she turns and walks off. I want to run after her and refuse to let her leave, but this is her choice. And she doesn't want me.

She loved me once, but she doesn't anymore. She said it herself. *She doesn't want me*.

I loved her back then, and I never stopped. I won't ever stop loving her. I don't know how.

As I watch her walk away, following a bit behind, just to make sure she's safe till she gets to the main road, I know one thing is true.

I don't wanna stop loving her. Ever. I don't know how I can move on.

CHAPTER 13

VIOLET

*T*he next day, I'm still cursing myself. Last night I went home and cried myself to sleep, wondering how the hell I could be so stupid.

I let Hunter kiss me. I let him woo me. I almost let him *fuck* me.

Almost.

Thank God he said those words, just like our first time together.

I want you, Vi.

Those words sent me straight back in time, like the last four years hadn't happened at all. As if he'd never gone to war, never thrown me away…

But he did. He did, damn it, and I don't know how to forget it.

So I left, ran in fact. My tears flowed freely, and kept right on until I fell asleep.

Now I'm at the bakery, and there are no tears in my eyes, but I still feel like a fool. I'm supposed to be older and wiser than I was four years ago, so why am I falling for the same old tricks?

Just because someone says they love you doesn't make it so. No matter how desperately you want it to be true.

I sigh and put another batch of cookies in the oven. I realize I'm feeling sorry for myself, but I can't seem to stop.

The door chimes. I look at the clock.

"Mail's here!"

I poke my head out and see the post lady, Gladys. She's got beautiful features and dark skin, which makes the blue of her postal uniform look awesome. She's been our mail carrier for years.

Still, her level of physical fitness for her age is something I aspire to.

"Hey," I say, greeting her as I walk to the front, carrying on with my life as if I'm not a complete wreck. "Whatcha got for me?"

"Just for you," she says with a wink.

She hands me a thick pile of mail. I smile, and offer her something from the display case.

"Anything you want," I say. "Got to keep our postal worker energized, you know."

"You're too good to me," she says. "How about one of those croissants?"

"You got it," I say, wrapping the croissant in a sheet of pastry paper.

I hand it to her and as usual, she tries to pull out her wallet.

"As if I'm ever going to take your money," I say with a smirk.

"Well, let it be known that I tried to pay," she says, her eyes sparkling. "Sometimes it's good to go through the motions, you know?"

She hefts her mail pouch, and I nod. That's what I've been doing all day, just going through the motions.

"I appreciate it, Gladys. See you tomorrow."

She shoots me a smile and heads out the door. My eyes fall to the pile of mail in my hands. I can tell without opening any of it that it's mostly bills.

I walk to the back, flipping through the stack. Water, electricity, credit cards, bulk orders of flour and dairy... The amount I owe is looking pretty substantial.

I try not to cringe as I set the bills down on my purse in the back of the room. If the bank doesn't approve my loan soon, I won't be able to cover them. And by soon, I mean within the week. It's been over the ten days they said it would take.

The door chimes again, so I leave the bills behind and head out front. To my surprise it's Slade, dressed in casual clothes. When I see him, I slow my steps. I didn't return his last two phone calls; I'm not interested. Or I wasn't, back when I thought I could give Hunter a chance. But I can't.

"Violet," Slade says, bringing my eyes back to his.

I just assumed that he would've given up on me by now, but here he is.

"Hey," I say, staying behind the counter.

"Hey," he says. He gestures to his clothes. "I knocked off work

102

a little early."

"I see that," I say, pinching my lips together. I'm pretty irritated with him, and coming into my shop expecting... whatever... isn't making it any better. It's almost five, but still. I don't like it.

You still need the loan, I remind myself. *So be nice.* I bite my tongue and try to give him a smile. I don't try too hard though, I'm just not right today and if he doesn't like it, he can fuck off.

"Listen, I know you're busy with... this," he says, waving his hands to indicate my shop. "But I bet you have time for a bite to eat."

"Slade..." I say, impatient but trying to hide it.

"C'mon. Let's just go to the diner," he says. "I'm buying."

He sounds almost charming, if I was into that kind of thing.

I purse my lips and think of all the bills in the back room. They aren't going anywhere anytime soon, and if one little meal could mean I get the loan...

"Okay," I say, slipping my apron over my head. "Let me get my purse and lock up." Just like Gladys said, I'm just going through the motions. At least that's what I tell myself.

Slade grins. I can tell he thinks he's irresistible. I try not to roll my eyes as I head to the back to gather my purse.

You can do this. It's just a meal, like he said. Not a date, like what I had with Hunter. This is nothing like that. My heart hurts, thinking about last night and our date.

I blow out a breath and head out front, trying to ignore all the emotions threatening to surface.

CHAPTER 14

HUNTER

I send another text to Jared. I've been bugging the shit out of him, but I don't care. I need to get the hell out of here and make myself useful. I've been home for two weeks and I haven't done a damn thing, except watch the one woman I ever loved walk away from me.

I look down at my phone. The text is sent, but he hasn't answered.

He has a life and responsibilities. I don't have shit.

We're gonna meet up later to look at this garage on West Avenue. It's a little rundown, but there's plenty of need for a mechanic shop in this town and that location is perfect.

Besides, I need to focus on something. I can't get over the fact that Vi doesn't want me. I can't stay in this fucking house, feeling sorry for myself.

I paid the down payment for a house on the outskirts of town today. I was eyeing it last week, but this morning I got my ass out there and settled on it. It's on a lake and in rough shape. That's good though. It'll keep me busy. I need that right now.

I'm distracted by the sound of high heels clicking against the old wooden floor.

Haley walks down the stairs wearing a dress that barely covers her ass. She's going out again.

Un-fucking-believable. Abbi's already in bed for a nap, but still I can't take it. I'm pissed.

I know she's single. I know she's getting over Chris' death. But she should have more respect than that. For herself, for her daughter, for the love she shared with Chris.

"Hey Hunter, I've gotta--"

She starts giving me the same shit she's been dishing out.

"Another date?"

My voice is hard when I cut her off. She flinches slightly before putting that bitchy facade back into place. She puts her hands on her hips and throws daggers at me.

I knew that she would. She has a right to be mad, and to deal with his death how she wants. But I can't keep quiet and not say anything anymore. She can fucking hate me if she wants.

"Yeah, I do, and I--"

"You need to knock it off, Haley." Jared's been talking to me about what the women are saying at Krissy's school. I don't fucking like hearing my sister's name in bad taste. Worse, I don't like that what they're saying is true. I know she's in pain, but she's only hurting herself more.

She opens her mouth and pinches her brows with disbelief. After a moment she points her finger at me even as her eyes glass over.

"You don't get to tell me what to do," she sneers.

"You're a grown ass woman and if you acted like it, I'd treat you like one. But you need to knock this shit off." I gesture to her outfit. "You have a little girl upstairs. Would you want her dealing with her pain the way you are?"

The mention of Abbi is a low blow, but it's about time I brought her up. She's got a life with Abbi. A good one. One she should be proud of. She's got money from Chris' death that she could use to get a house of her own, and that could help her move on. But she hasn't done shit with the money, except buy these clothes that barely fucking fit her.

Haley looks hurt for a moment, then turns slightly to look over her shoulder as my father walks into the room.

Yet another member of my family that I'm pissed at. I'm just pissed at everyone, it seems.

He crosses his arms and leans against the doorway, but doesn't say anything. He should say something, though. This family never talks about a damn thing. I'm ready to talk, and they better be ready to listen.

Haley turns back to look at me and lowers her voice.

"You have no idea what it's like," she swallows thickly before continuing, "I lost the one man…"

Her voice cracks, and her shoulders hunch forward. I get up from the sofa and wrap her in my arms. She starts to push me away, her heels clicking loudly on the old wooden floor, but her gesture is weak.

"Let it out," I say, gently rubbing her back. She tries to say something, tries to push me away, but she breaks down in my arms.

She loses it. She sobs into my chest. It's been close to nine months now since Chris passed. Nine months of misery, of trying to navigate grief.

Nine months can be a long time, or a short time. But it doesn't make it hurt any less. Sometimes it feels so long and guilt weighs against my chest that I could be moving on without him. Sometimes it's been too soon and I can't do a damn thing without hearing his voice in my head.

Tears still cloud my own eyes when I remember him. I was their best man. I'll never forget how happy he was. Happy to be married to Haley, and happy for her to be carrying his baby girl.

Chris was a good man, and it's terrible that Haley and Abbi lost him. I wish I could bring him back. But I can't.

"I know, Haley. I know it hurts."

She shakes her head, ruffling her hair, but doesn't say anything.

"I do know. I was there, and I couldn't do anything. I wish I could. I wish I could take it all back. I would, Haley. I'd take his place for you if I could."

"Don't say that," she says weakly, not looking me in the eyes. I run my hand up and down her arm, holding her close.

"You gotta take care of yourself and Abbi, Haley. You gotta try to move on."

"I can't, Hunter," Haley whimpers in my chest and pulls away, wiping under her eyes.

"You can, baby girl," my father says. He walks over and rubs her back.

She takes in a ragged breath and gives him a hug, too. All the while he's looking me in the eyes.

"Go on upstairs. I think you should stay in and maybe take a while to think about things?" Pops tells her.

She doesn't argue as she walks away, taking in steadying breaths.

Pops watches her walk away. I don't wait for him to say a damn word to me. I don't need his advice. I'm pent up and feeling like shit. I need to get out of here.

I need Vi. I know with everything in me that I need her.

The sky's a dark grey, making it feel later than it is. It's spitting out rain and I can hear faint thunder coming in.

I hear my father yell out my name, but I don't stop. I look over my shoulder as I open the door to the truck and see him standing on the porch, but I have nothing to say to him right now.

I hop in my truck without looking back. I try to push away the memories of Chris. The tires squeal on the wet road as I speed off to go see Vi.

I just need her. I don't know what for, but right now I know I need my Vi. If she won't have me as a lover, I'll settle for a friend. I can only hope she'll let me in. I need her.

I told Chris about her. He made a big deal of telling me I was a fucking idiot for throwing away what I had with her.

I pinch the bridge of my nose as I pull up to the red light at the end of the street and try to prevent the tears pricking my eyes from coming through at the memory.

I remember how he laughed at me. He said one day I'd see what a mistake I'd made. He was right. Fuck, I wish he was here now so I could tell him. I bang my fist on the steering wheel, hating what time has done to me.

I breathe out slow and steady and keep the bitch tears from surfacing as I pull up into the bakery parking lot.

Her car's not there. Where the hell is she?

I pull in and get out, walking around the side where she came in the other night. The rain comes down a little harder, and the light in the sky dims.

I knock against her door with my fist. It's clenched so tight, I think the skin will break with each pounding knock.

I need someone to lean on, and I want that someone to be Vi. But she's not here.

I scream out her name and back up a few steps to look in her window. But it's pointless. She's gone. I don't know where, but she's not here.

My phone beeps in my pocket. The sky cracks with an angry bolt of lightning and the rain comes down harder, pounding against my head and shoulders, soaking my clothes.

I get in the truck and slam the door. I'm drenched, and somehow feeling worse than I did when I left.

I pull the phone from my pocket and look down, hoping it's Vi like the fucking idiot that I am.

It's a text from Jared.

. . .

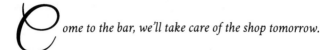 *ome to the bar, we'll take care of the shop tomorrow.*

I start up the car and try not to think about Vi or where she is right now.

A drink is exactly what I need.

CHAPTER 15

I follow Slade and the redheaded waitress through the diner, looking at the sagging blue plastic seats and chipped white laminate tables. The second we walked out of my bakery, I knew this was a mistake.

To go on a date with Slade after letting Hunter hold me close, kiss me so thoroughly…

Technically, it wasn't *wrong* or *slutty*, but it kind of felt that way. Especially with Slade putting his hands all over me and wrapping his arm around my waist. I'm trying not to be a bitch, but I don't like it.

I sigh silently as Slade examines several booths before choosing one, totally ignoring the waitress. I realize I'm going to have to tell Slade I don't want to date him, as soon as I find out whether or not I get the loan. Which better happen… like now.

"Which one do you want?" Slade asks, frowning at the tables.

"Doesn't matter," I say, crossing my arms. It's a booth. All the tables are flat, so I don't give a fuck.

He looks at me and sees how impatient I am, so he relents. "Alright. How about this one?"

"Fine," I say, choosing a side of the table and sitting down. I toss my purse down next to me onto the booth.

"Great," he says, scootching into my side of the table. "Move over, will you?"

I picture a gleaming new oven as I move over to accommodate him. *Is it worth it?* I wonder.

"Here you go!" the waitress says, handing us menus. "Can I get you something to drink?"

Before I can open my mouth, Slade cuts in.

"She'll have a diet soda, and I'll have coffee," he says.

I frown as the waitress skips off to put the order in. As if he didn't really just order for me. My mouth opens and closes, with nothing coming out for a moment. I close my eyes and calm myself down. I'm just worked up, that's all this is.

"I hate diet soda," I inform him. "It tastes like plastic."

"Well, I think it's time you start expanding your palate a little," he says, looking at the menu. "After all, you won't be thin forever. My father says self-maintenance is best done before there's an issue."

I scowl down at my menu. I'm a little surprised, but not as much as I should be. I opt to say nothing, since his comment is so offhanded, but inside I've gone from being blasé to being downright pissed.

Slade seems oblivious. He launches into a long, boring story about a meeting he had at the bank with an awkward client. It's only when he's wrapping the story up because the waitress is returning with our drinks, that I realize he just told me about declining someone's loan. About how fun it was for him, how funny it was.

I glance at him, flustered.

"A coffee for you, and a diet soda for the lady," the redhead says.

"Thanks," I mumble. "Actually, could I just get a water?"

Slade's look is approving, which makes me want to order ten milkshakes, but I stay mum.

New oven. New oven, I remind myself. *You can do it.*

"Sure thing! Do you guys know what you want to order?" the waitress asks, pulling out a pad of paper and a pen.

I expect Slade to allow me to order first, but he doesn't. Instead, he orders *for* me.

"She'll have the house salad, no croutons, dressing on the side," he says. "And I'll have a BLT with fries."

The waitress writes everything down, despite the fact that my jaw is hanging open with shock. I'm a human, not a fucking rabbit.

"Anything else?" she asks, barely looking up.

"I—" I say, but Slade cuts me off.

"No thanks," he says, grabbing the menu out of my hands and stacking it with the other one.

"I'll have that right out for you," the redhead says, blushing when she makes eye contact with Slade. She bobs him a curtsy as she scoops up the menus. "Sir."

As soon as she's gone, I turn to Slade.

"You don't order for me," I say, keeping my words measured. "Ever."

"Oh, come on," he says, waving his hand. "I ordered you what my father gets for my mother. It's a *gesture*."

I stare at him, befuddled. He honestly thinks I want him to choose my food for me? The part about his parents doesn't escape me, either.

He thinks this is getting serious, I realize. *This is normal behavior for him.*

Slade immediately changes the story, telling me instead all of the things he's heard about the young woman who's waiting on us. I look at him blankly.

There's no way he can think that I'm interested in this, right? This just reminds me that I'm the subject of their gossip when I'm not looking. At that thought, I'm done. I don't give a fuck if my life is ruined over not getting this damn loan. I. Am. Done.

"Can I get out?" I blurt.

Slade looks a little surprised that I interrupted him in the middle of a sentence. How *rude* of me.

"Uh... okay," he says, disgruntled.

He makes a show of folding his napkin and putting it on the table, then sliding out of the booth. I get out of the booth, rummaging around in my purse. I refuse to owe him anything, even if he promised to pay for the meal.

"Here," I say, offering him a twenty. "To cover my meal."

I turn away and start to leave, but he stops me, his hand banding around my forearm. He jerks me so that I'm off balance when I look back at him. The pinch hurts my arm a bit, and my hand instinctively flies to his to get him off of me.

"Sit. Down." His words are hissed.

"No," I say, tugging on my arm to free myself.

He doesn't let go, though. He draws me closer, his eyes burning into mine.

"I said sit down," he says. "There's no reason to cause a scene."

"Stop it, Slade," I say, my voice gone to gravel. "Let me go."

A furious look comes over his face. "Outside, *now*."

He starts dragging me toward the exit by the arm, oblivious to the fact that the waitress is staring at him with something like horror.

He's squeezing so hard that it hurts, so hard that my arm goes a little numb. It feels like a bruising hold and my heartbeat speeds up, hating that he won't let me go.

"Now!" he growls, giving me a hard shake.

I stop resisting, nearly paralyzed with shock and fear. Slade manages to pull me outside as my blood heats and I try to wrap my head around what's going on. A sea-change has come over him as he yanks me around the side of the building, away from prying eyes.

He's red in the face, sweating, and he doesn't mind getting in my face. So close that his hot breath hits me, and makes my neck arch away from him.

"Where do you think you're gonna go, huh?" he says, pushing me against the building. My back hits the cold brick wall and I gasp. "Do you think there's somewhere you can go that I don't control? Somewhere you can run around and be a slut, embarrass me?"

"Slade—" I try to speak, barely managing to get his name out of my mouth.

"You shut up. You're good enough to look at, and you have childbearing hips," he says, releasing my arm to grab my hips. "And my father says you pass muster. So I'm going to train you, teach you how to be a wife."

I open my mouth again to protest, but he kisses me roughly, covering my mouth with his and shoving his tongue down my throat. His hands tear at my blouse, and I'm afraid that he'll rip it. I push my hands against his shoulders, trying to push him away, but he only moves in closer, as if to show me how weak I am.

"St-" I move my face away from his to tell him no, but he grips my jaw and crushes his lips against mine.

I'm afraid he'll do more than that, actually. I struggle, but it only seems to excite him. I try to push him away, but I'm too weak. I try to scream, but the sounds are muffled by his mouth on mine. My breathing comes in frantic pants, and my heart beats so hard it hurts. One of his hands snakes down between us, intent on getting up my skirt.

I don't know what happens, exactly, but that's some kind of trigger. Just before he can touch my panties, I shove him back with all my weight. He laughs and comes at me again, but this time I'm ready for him.

I knee him in the balls as hard as I can, right between the legs.

His face would be comical if I wasn't so panicked. I don't stick around for him to recover, though.

I turn toward the front of the building and *run*.

CHAPTER 16

HUNTER

"**S**o you fucked it up," Jared says matter-of-factly.

I grip the bar top and groan with frustration. I look at him seated on the barstool to my right, waiting for the punch line. But there is none.

I look at him straight faced as he brings the beer to his lips. "That's not at all what I said." He laughs into it and then takes a swig.

The college game is on the TVs on the front wall, and I can hear the cheers from them in the background. There are a few guys in here; Casey and Sean I know, but there are a a few older guys I don't. The retirees are watching the game, while Casey and Sean are in the back playing pool with someone else.

I've spent a good forty minutes trying to explain to Jared what the hell's going on with Vi, and all he keeps saying is that I fucked it up.

"How did I fuck up?" I wish he'd just tell me. I don't care

what I've gotta do to make it right.

"She didn't forgive you," he says, tilting his beer and taking another swig.

"Yeah, I know that, but how the fuck is that my fault?"

He looks at me with a straight face. "The first thing you should know is that it's always your fault."

Sean's behind us and he lets out a small grunt of a laugh. I turn to look at him, and he's leaning against the wall holding the pool stick and nodding his head as he watches Casey take another shot.

"Okay," I say and try to contain my anger. I set my beer down. "So how do I make her forgive me?" 'Cause that's what I really want. That's my end game. They can joke about me fucking up all they want as long as they give me a game plan on how to win her back.

Jared shrugs.

"I don't know, man." He tosses his empty beer behind the bar and into an oversized trash can. He makes the shot, but the old bartender looks up and glares at him. Jared raises his hands in defeat, but the smirk on his face doesn't dim.

"I think she just needs time," he finally says.

"She's had years to forgive me." I run my hands through my hair in frustration. "How long can she possibly stay mad?"

"No," he says with a hard edge. "You just came back." He stares at me with his brows furrowed. "She's only just finding out how you really feel."

I groan in frustration and lay my head on the bar.

"I know. But I'm here now."

I know I could make everything right, but she's not giving me a chance. I sigh, feeling defeated. I want my Vi back. I don't want her to stay mad at me forever. I want her to *want* me again.

"Give the girl some time," the bartender says. I think I heard one of the other guys call him Ralph earlier. He's old and has a wedding band on his ring finger. I make a point to take advice from people who have what I want. Maybe I do just need to give her time. Ralph opens another bottle and sets it down in front of me. I pass him my empty one and nod my head.

But damn, I don't want to give her time. I want her *now*.

The cold beer feels good going down. I guess a little time won't hurt anything. I can get my shit together, and be a man worth having. I can become the man who belongs next to her.

"How long?" I ask with impatience.

I lean back on the barstool so the front feet leave the ground, and I'm balancing with my boots pushing against the bar.

The guys behind me start laughing again, and then someone scores on the TV. The guy on the other end of the bar hollers out and salutes the bartender with his beer before taking a long drink. The bartender looks at the TV with disdain, shaking his head.

"I don't know why I make bets with you, Earl," Ralph mutters while keeping his eyes on the game.

"Uh, Hunter. Ain't that your girl out there?" Casey asks, looking out the window with his pool stick in his hand.

I snap my weight forward, so I don't fall, and I go over to the window.

I squint and spot Vi running. What the fuck is she doing?

She's running down the empty sidewalk. It's hard to make her out in between the lamp posts.

All the stores are closed except for the bar and a few restaurants down the street. But as soon as she passes under the bright light, I know it's her. Her blouse is pulled out of her waist, and her hair looks disheveled. What the fuck?

My heart pounds in my chest.

Adrenaline pumps in my blood as I take off out of the bar. I push the door open so hard it smacks into the brick building with a loud crack. I don't care though.

"Vi!" I call out for her as I take off in her direction.

She sees me, and it spurs her onward, toward me. Tears are streaming down her face.

She's breathing heavy. She doesn't stop for one second to come right into my open arms.

She takes in a ragged breath and buries her head in my chest. I wish I could enjoy the fact that she's finding comfort in my embrace, that I happened to be here at the right time and place, but something's wrong. Something upset her and made her afraid.

I hear Jared come up behind me. "Is she alright?" he asks.

A few other guys are behind him, wondering what the hell is going on. They're all looking at her, and she's just trying to hide in my arms.

"Vi, what's wrong?" I ask her softly, my lips brushing against her hair.

She doesn't answer me, but she looks up. She goes stiff in my arms as she sees the guys staring at her.

Jared comes a little closer and takes a look at her.

"You alright?" he asks.

A few other people have gathered across the street from the pizza shop. My anxiety spikes, seeing how everyone's coming out to see what's going on.

"Talk to me," I tell her.

Vi seems more settled and she pulls away, realizing that I'm holding her. She takes a few steps back and hugs herself.

She looks around, and her face shows the pain she's in. She doesn't want people seeing her like this, and I get that. But she needs to tell me what the hell happened.

She looks a bit cold so I take my jacket off and try to give it to her, but she doesn't take it. She shakes her head and sniffles a bit, wiping under her eyes.

"I'm fine," she says weakly.

She's not fine, she's anything but fine. I open my mouth to tell her that, but then I see that fucker Slade jogging up the street.

He stops when he sees us, but I can make out enough. His disheveled appearance and pissed off expression tell me what I need to know.

I know he hurt her. And that's all I need to know. I'm about to make this asshole pay for what he did.

I wrap my coat around Vi, ignoring her protests. I look back at Jared as I take a step around her and head to Slade.

"Watch her," I tell him.

I take a final look at Violet as she turns and sees what's about to happen.

"Hunter, no!" she yells out weakly and reaches for me, but that's not gonna work.

No one's gonna hurt my girl and get away with it.

CHAPTER 17

VIOLET

*H*unter throws his jacket around my shoulders, and it's only then that I realize I'm trembling. I don't know if it's because it's so cold, or if it's because I'm so emotionally taxed. I try to tell him I don't need it, even though the warmth of his jacket feels soothing on my shoulders, but then I look at Hunter, and his eyes aren't on me at all and the words stall in my throat.

He's looking past me. I turn and see Slade, slowing his steps and looking pissed as hell. My heart hammers faster and I grip onto Hunter's arm, but he pulls away from me and refuses to listen.

"Hunter, don't," I say, taking a few steps to keep up with him.

"Watch her," Hunter orders someone behind me and I try grabbing him again, but it's too late.

I get a flash of intuition when I see Hunter look at Slade, and I know that they're going to fight. There's no stopping this. I take in a ragged breath as Jared stops me from running after

Hunter. His arms wrap around me, and I slap him away. I can't tear my eyes away from Hunter. I can hardly breathe. I don't want this. I don't want him to fight over me.

Slade's stopped walking, and he yells something at Hunter that I can't quite make out.

"Hunter, no!" I scream, but he doesn't listen.

Jared's holding me loosely and I shove him once, and that's all it takes. He releases me but as soon as I take a step closer, intent on keeping the two of them apart, Jared grabs my hand.

"Violet, don't get yourself in the middle." His voice is low and apologetic.

Hunter charges at Slade, a roar escaping his throat. I stare after Hunter, and witness Slade square off in preparation. This isn't good.

"Hunter!" I yell, but Hunter keeps going, barreling into Slade.

Hunter and Slade are already throwing punches at each other, frenzied.

I look around at the people who are starting to gather. I realize that most of the watchers are oscillating between watching the fight and looking to see my reaction.

It reminds me of four years ago; the gossip then was about what I had done wrong, why I hadn't gotten Hunter to propose to me, how I had to live in shame after he left.

It's unfair, how it's always the woman's fault.

If he would just listen to me. I pull away from Jared, but make no move to go to Hunter.

I feel myself turning red, feel my neck growing hot. This is so embarrassing.

Damn them all. They're soaking up gossip, material they'll use to talk down to me. I bite my lip, moving toward Hunter and Slade. I just want them to stop fighting, but no one's stepping in to break it up.

"Jared," I say and catch his eyes. "Do something," I plead with him.

He looks at the two of them. Hunter's on top of Slade now, beating the shit out of him. His hands clench into fists, but he just shakes his head at me.

I grit my teeth. I realize I'll have to be the one to break up the fight.

The next minute goes so fast, I'm barely aware of its passing.

I dart forward in the second that they pull apart, wiping their bloodied faces. I try to get between them, to push them apart.

Instead, Hunter goes for Slade's throat, elbowing me in the side of the head. One second I'm moving toward Hunter, the next I'm spinning away. Fuck!

I hit the pavement hard, scraping my arm and feeling a pain radiating in my temple. Damn, that hurt. It takes a second before I'm able to breathe and reach my hand up to the side of my head. I wince when my fingers touch where Hunter landed the blow.

I prop myself up slightly and ignore the pain, looking up at the two men who are fighting over me. Or were fighting — now that they've knocked me down, they're concerned about me again.

"Vi—"

"Violet!"

I wipe at my lip and glance at the crowd. The reaction seems to be somewhere between horror and shock, and I feel crushed beneath their curious gazes.

Hunter grabs my arm and hauls me to my feet.

"I'm sorry," he says, looking at me like a piece of fragile china. "I didn't mean to, I swear. Are you okay?"

Slade is on my other side, shoving Hunter off.

"Don't you touch her," Slade says loud enough for everyone to hear and trying to wrap his arm around my shoulders. He's got a busted lip and he wipes away the blood with the back of his shirt sleeve.

I can't stop looking at the gathered audience, whispering. I'm completely overwhelmed.

Once again, it's me that will be the subject of rampant gossip, me that will bear the burden of what happened today.

Enough.

"Get off," I say to Hunter, my pitch sharp. I look at Slade. "And you, too. Both of you just get off of me."

I shake them both off, and start running toward my apartment above the bakery. I'm so ashamed, miserable with it. Tears stream down my face, though I didn't notice them until now.

Both Hunter and Slade are adding to my burden, to the gossip about me, and I won't have it. Can't deal with it.

"Vi! Violet—" Hunter calls, but I ignore him.

I keep running, hoping that I can outrun my past, outrun all the damage done.

Maybe if I keep going, it will work this time.

CHAPTER 18

HUNTER

*I*t's silent in the empty police station. Just me and the sheriff. I can feel his eyes on me, but I don't look up. I wrap the gauze around my knuckles and do my best to calm the fuck down. The adrenaline is still racing in my blood.

I wasn't done with Slade when Vi got in the middle. She shouldn't have done that. I wish she hadn't. Even worse, I struck her. I pulled back and slammed my elbow into her. I know it hurt. My poor Vi. I don't know what the hell she was thinking.

I stood there, watching her run from me. Literally running. My heart's never hurt so damn much. I don't wanna cause her pain. Ever. And I keep fucking doing it.

I could hear the sirens and the blood rushing in my ears as I watched her leave me.

I stretch my jaw. My lip's split, and I'm sure I'll have a bruise on my cheek by the way it feels. He hit me back once, maybe twice. But as soon as I got on top of him and started laying into him, all he did was try to block my punches.

I still don't know what he did to her. If the cops hadn't shown up the second I lost her in my vision, I would've beat the piss out of him until he told me.

Vi didn't say a damn thing to anyone, as far as I know. She didn't tell me or anyone else what he did, but that bastard said enough for me to figure out he hurt her.

I can still hear him screaming how she's a liar and she wanted it when I started walking toward him. That was what sent me over the edge. That's what pushed me to charge at that fucker. My fist clenches, and the blood soaks through the bandages.

I look down at my hand and slowly pull the ruined bandages away. I can still feel his bones crunching beneath my heavy blows to his face.

Black eyes and a broken nose aren't enough. But at least I put some damage on him before Sheriff Caswell showed up.

"Mr. White wants to press charges," the sheriff says from where he's standing a few feet away.

I hear the sheriff talking, but I don't look up. I huff a humorless laugh and ball up the gauze, tossing it into the small trash bin in the corner of the police station.

We're in the front room, by the desk. It's a narrow hall really. The cells are in the back. At least he didn't put me back there... yet.

"What about the charges Violet's gonna press against him?"

I see his boots shift on the ground, and he hesitates to answer. I look up at the old man with a hard expression.

She better get justice. More than what I can give her.

"He says he didn't do anything to her," he replies, and his soft blue eyes stare down at me with sadness. His voice is low, but even.

"And what'd she say?" I ask.

My voice cracks a bit, making me sound weak. But that's how I feel. I don't like the way Sheriff Caswell's looking at me. I get a sense that nothing's gonna come from this.

They've gotta believe her. Caswell's a good man. This town is full of good people. They'll stand by her, I know they will.

"Nothing," he answers me. His eyes are pleading with me for something. But I don't know what.

Nothing? I don't understand.

I sit back on the bench and run my hand through my hair. I can't look at him. I stare at the anti-drug posters on the back wall.

Finally I look at him, as my body heats with anxiety and my heart slows.

"What do you mean, nothing?"

"She didn't want to talk. She answered questions about the fight, but she didn't want to talk about anything else."

I lean forward with my head in my hands; my gut twists and my heart clenches. My Vi. My poor Vi.

My eyes feel glassy with tears, but I shove that down and look up at him. "She's just hurting."

"I know. That doesn't change the fact that she's not pressing charges, but Slade's pressing them on you."

My body goes tense, and I grit my teeth.

"Slade got what he had coming to him."

My voice is low as I push out the words. My muscles flex, and I resist the urge to get up and do something stupid, like rip this place apart.

The anger is good though. I know how to handle my anger. It's the pain I feel for Vi that I don't know what to do with.

"I don't disagree. I do have some questions to ask you though."

I nod my head once and wait for it. I'm mostly waiting for him to cuff me and throw me in a cell.

"We have several conflicting testimonies. Some say you hit him first, others say he hit you first." My brows raise, and I stay still as a wave of shock hits me. "Now, obviously if you were to admit that you hit him first, he'd have reasonable cause and I'd be forced to arrest you, son."

He pauses, and I wait for him to continue. I did hit him first, and I'm not gonna lie about that.

"But if you didn't, then... I don't see a reason that he could file charges."

I stare at my hands, not wanting to lie. But I sure as fuck don't wanna sit behind bars while Vi is God knows where. She needs me.

"What if I don't say anything?" I ask him.

"Then I think I'd tell you to get your ass home and stay outta trouble."

I nod my head and stand up. He doesn't need to tell me twice, and I don't need to give him time to change his mind.

As I walk to the front door, he says, "Just keep your head down and your mouth shut about it."

I nod my head and mutter that I will. Slade better stay away though.

"I won't be able to help you again," Sheriff Caswell warns.

"I hear ya." As long as Slade stays away from Vi, we won't have any problems. And after the ass whooping I gave him, I can't imagine he'll be coming back for seconds.

"And about Violet," the sheriff says as I open the door. I turn to look at him over my shoulder. "I'll be here when she wants to talk."

I maintain eye contact with him and nod. "Thank you, Sheriff."

The cold breeze of the early morning whips across my face. It's fucking cold. I'm tired, feeling like shit, and hating everything that just happened. I start walking to the bar's parking lot and then realize I don't have the keys to my truck. They're in my coat pocket, the coat I gave Vi last night.

At least I have a legitimate reason to see her then. Even if she doesn't wanna talk, even if she doesn't want to see me.

I just wanna know she's alright. That's the only thing that matters right now.

CHAPTER 19

VIOLET

I walk up the driveway of my parents' house with a heavy heart, knowing I have to tell my mama I'm leaving. I let myself into the house, feeling like a quitter. I came here instead of going home. It's closer, but that's not why I came here. I need my mama.

"Hello?" I call out from the foyer.

"In here!" Mama calls out.

I follow her voice and head into the living room, where she's propped up in her favorite recliner under a ton of blankets. She hits mute on the TV remote and turns to me with the ghost of a smile.

My first thought is that she doesn't look good. She looks pinched and grey.

"Hey Mama," I say, walking over to drop a kiss on her cheek. "Whatcha watching?"

"Oh, some antiques show," she says, waving her hand. "It's not important."

"Ah," I say, taking the chair beside hers. "Where's Dad?"

"He's at the Elks Lodge, drinking dollar beers and hustling fellow members at pool."

I try to relax into the seat, but I'm tense. I've got a bit of blood on the sleeve of my shirt from where Hunter grabbed me, but other than that I look normal. I think. I'm nervous and anxious to tell her what happened.

Especially since it seems like she's having a bad day today, healthwise. I hate the idea that my leaving will have an effect on her, though I know it will. At least no one called to tell her first. Or if they called, she didn't answer. I have to tell her before they do. I can't let her find out about things that way.

When I finally work up the will to tell her, I look over at her. She's looking back at me with compassion, the kind of feeling that can't be invented or faked.

Despite all my best intentions, I burst into tears.

"Ohhh, my girl," she says, reaching out to pat my hand. "It's not so bad, my darling."

Her words only make me cry harder, because I know that she's wrong. It is bad. It's unlivable.

"The bakery—" I start, then stop to get my tears under control. "The bakery is going to go under, Mama. And I can't get a loan to fix the oven because Slade and his father run the bank. Even before, when Slade wasn't mad at me, I don't think I could've gotten the loan. And then Slade tried to force me to…"

I stop, and take in air in big gulps. I'm panicking, telling my mama too much, but I have to tell *someone*. It all just keeps spilling out.

"What did Slade do?" Mama asks, her voice going hard.

"Slade tried to force himself on me, and so I ran. And of course I ran right into Hunter, and Hunter attacked Slade. I got in between them, and got knocked to the ground. And there were all these people there who were watching..." I trail off and sob.

"Honey," my mama says, moving so I'm closer. I lean my head against her chair, anguished. "I know you're struggling right now. Your father and I can pay for the oven..."

I sit up, wiping at my face. She misunderstood me.

"No, Mama. I'm trying to tell you... I'm trying to say I have to leave Hallow Falls."

Mama's eyes narrow on my face, but she doesn't disagree with me. Her next words are tender.

"Are you sure you're running toward your dream? You're not just running away from your fears?" she asks carefully.

"I just... I need to get away from this town. And Hunter, and Slade..." I can't finish that train of thought. I breathe in deep and says, "I want to be a teacher, you know? I'm not meant to be running the bakery, it just sort of fell into my lap. It was never a part of my plan." I wipe at my blotchy face, though I've finally stopped crying. "I need to start over, to get a clean slate."

My mama looks at me for a second, her eyes welling with tears.

"Don't cry," I tell her. "Or I'll start again."

"Just... just follow your heart, baby," my mama says, brushing back a strand of my hair. "That's all you can do."

I take a deep breath and blow it out.

"I'm not leaving right now," I say, covering my mama's hand with my own. "Okay? I'll stick around a little longer. I just know I need to get out, and I know you're the reason I stay."

"Well, you don't have to stay because of me," she sighs. "You don't stay here for me, you hear?"

"Okay, Mama."

"You just go when you're ready, alright? You let me and your father know where you're going, but other than that… don't worry about me."

I halfheartedly smile at her and nod, and my mama pats my shoulder. I don't have anything more to say.

My mama turns the sound up on whatever show she was watching, and I slide deeper into my seat. We sit like that for a long while, until she falls asleep.

CHAPTER 20

I've been waiting against the side of Vi's bakery since 5 a.m.; when the sheriff let me leave, I walked straight here. My boots and ass are in the dirt and my back's against the cement wall. It's cold as fuck and there's not a goddamn thing around here to do. I would've fallen asleep from exhaustion if I wasn't so fucking pissed and worried.

I don't have my phone or my keys. But more than that, I don't know where Vi is. She could be anywhere. I'm hoping she's at a friend's house.

But all sorts of bullshit has been running through my mind for the last few hours. I wanna know where she is. And I'm coming up with all sorts of places, but I keep settling on Slade's house. And not because she wants to be there. A few times I almost walked over to his parents' house. I don't know where Slade's is, but if he'd gotten his hands on her, I wouldn't have let anyone pry me away from him again.

I know where she is now; she's walking my way with wide,

worried eyes. I get up off the ground, brushing the dirt off my ass and feeling sore all over.

She's wearing the clothes she was in last night, and they're wrinkled like she slept in them. Her eyes are red and slightly swollen and her face is tearstained. *Vi.*

"You weren't here last night." My voice comes out harder than I intended. "Where were you?" I can't help how the words come out. That's the only thing on my mind.

She stops in her tracks and takes in a shaky breath. At first I think I startled her, but that's not it. She's pissed.

"It's none of your business. *I'm* none of your business. You made that clear all those years ago. Just leave me alone, Hunter." Her voice cracks on the last word. On my name.

I'm taken aback by her anger. "I just wanted to talk to you," I say in a soothing voice. She still hasn't moved. She's a mix of emotions, and I'm not sure what's winning out, but she's not okay.

"I don't need to talk to anyone. I'm done with this town, and I'm done with you, Hunter Graves." She shakes her head and says, "You're no good for me. There's nothing good for me here."

Although her voice is even, it's like she's slapped me. I don't understand what the fuck changed for her. Then it hits me. Slade.

Whatever that fucker did, it messed her up. She's not okay, and I'm gonna have to be gentle with her. But I can help her. I know I can.

She just has to let me in. I fucking hope she does. She needs me.

"What did I do, Vi?" I ask, taking a step toward her. She almost takes a step backward, but she stops herself.

"Don't, Hunter." She looks up at me with pleading eyes, and I listen to her. I stop, I put my hands up in surrender.

"I'm only here for you." I look back at her and take a moment to collect my thoughts. "I don't want you to run away from-"

"It's not running, Hunter." She lets out a long breath, trying to calm herself. It kills me to watch her and not give into the urge to take her in my arms like she needs.

"I think you are running," I say and she opens her mouth to object, but I keep going, "and I get it, Vi. I understand, and I'm so damn sorry. But you don't have to run."

"Let me hold you," I ask even though it's more of a command.

"No," she says, shaking her head and wrapping her arms around her. Her blouse bunches, and she looks away. She shakes her head, looking at the bushes that line this side of the building.

I give her a minute to calm down. She wipes under her eyes and lets her shoulders hunch forward.

"I'm here for you." I say the words softly. I just need her to believe it. All this other shit, I don't care about it. I don't live for it. But I live for her. Even with all those years away in the Navy and all the shit I got in, I just kept thinking I needed to get out and get back here. I had to get back to her. I wish she knew that. I wish she'd believe me.

She looks up at me, but she doesn't answer. It cuts me deep that she won't talk to me.

"Is this about Slade?" I ask softly. Her eyes flicker to the ground and she reaches up, hugging herself again. "What'd he do to you?"

She shakes her head, refusing to give me an inch. She looks so wounded. She's not the woman I know. I just need to know what happened so I can fix it.

"I'll kill him if he ever touches you again," I say with conviction in my voice.

Before I can say any more, her phone rings in her purse. At first she ignores it, but the ringtone is different. It must be someone important. Her forehead scrunches as she digs for it and then answers the call.

I can barely make out the sound of her father's voice.

She answers with a question in her voice, "Dad?"

Her face pales, and she covers her mouth with her hand, shaking her head. Fuck. I walk closer to her, trying to understand what's going on. Why she's so upset. I'm cautious, but then she loses it, and her phone falls to the ground.

I grab her small body in my arms before she collapses to the ground, with her shoulders trembling and tears flowing down her cheeks.

"Vi?" I'm desperate to understand what's wrong. I have no fucking clue. But she's not okay, she's hysterical.

I hold her, not knowing what's wrong and just trying to calm her down.

"Vi, what's wrong?" I pet her back and kiss her hair, waiting for her to tell me something.

She finally grabs a hold of me, burying her head in my chest. A sob wracks her body. "Vi?" I ask her again, but she just holds me tighter. I sit on the ground, holding her in my lap. "What happened?" I ask again, rocking her back and forth.

She sniffles and takes in a ragged breath, not pulling away from me. With her head still buried beneath my chin she manages to answer, and my heart shatters.

"My mama... she," she cries harder. "She died."

CHAPTER 21

I'm at my parents' house, just after the funeral, standing in the backyard. My mother's wake is still going on inside, but I need a break.

I'm still in my funeral clothes, a black lace dress and black pumps. I brush back a lock of my dark hair, frowning at how windy it is today.

That's the weather report today: windy, cool, and grey. I look up at the sky, wondering how the sky knew that it should be grey today.

When I was little, my mama used to say that grey days were God's way of keeping the sun fresh. The corners of my mouth curl up as I imagine my mama saying just that to a younger version of myself.

In my mind, my mama says it to me as I'm peering outside, looking glum. She turns me around and tucks a stray lock of hair behind my ear. Then she says, *Today is grey because God is keeping the sun fresh.*

It's a nice memory, as comforting to me as the smell of cinnamon and the warmth of the fireplace.

Then I realize that she'll never say that to me ever again. She'll never again say anything to me. She's said all that she'll ever say.

The pain is like a knife in my heart, the memory exposing yet another nerve ending to be sliced and shredded. This is about the thousandth time I've gone through this exact process since she died. Remembering something small but nice, reliving it, only for the whole thing to come crashing down. Crumpling my heart and causing me nothing but pain.

I sniffle and kick the dirt, trying to alleviate some of the emotion overwhelming me.

Reality sucks, big time.

I shiver and wrap my arms around myself, even though it isn't exactly cold. It's warmer than it has been lately. I look out into the woods behind my parents' house, trying not to cry.

I think I've cried myself out, anyway. I cried when my father told me that my mama died. I cried almost all day, every day between then and now. I cried when they put my mama in the ground.

That's a lot of crying, a lot of tears. I think my mama would've appreciated my efforts not to cry anymore, now that the funeral's over.

My mama is dead. She's gone. There is nothing on this earth that can bring her back. Nothing that can ease my pain.

It's midmorning, but I could do with some sleep. I've only

slept a handful of hours this whole week, but now it seems like all I wanna do is sleep.

Come to think of it, I don't think I've ever been as tired as I am right now.

The sliding glass door opens, and I turn to look at who decided to come join me out here. It's Hunter, looking somber in his dark suit and tie.

I don't think I've ever seen him in a suit. His broad shoulders fill the jacket and make him look... powerful. He looks like he owns the world wearing that suit. Or maybe just me. The sight of him, looking so polished and domineering, makes me want him. I look away at that realization. I don't want him. I can't.

"Vi," he says, his voice gone to gravel. "I came to see how you're doing."

I look at him. He was at the funeral, though he stayed on the edges of the crowd.

"Are you alright?" he asks, moving toward me.

I stay still as he takes one of my hands in his, squeezing it gently. I shake my head, tilting it down so that my dark hair covers my face.

He reads me immediately, just like he used to in high school.

"Hey," he says, touching my shoulder and then wrapping his arms around me. "It's okay, Violet. It's okay. You're not going to feel this way forever. I promise." It hurts to hear him say that. It doesn't feel that way. I can't imagine ever living a day without her and not feeling this pain and emptiness inside of me.

I close my eyes and revel in the comfort of his embrace for a moment. It's nice, feeling the simple comfort of his arms around me. It makes me yearn, makes me want more. I reach up and put my arms around his shoulders, letting him hold me. I melt into him and feel a desire for more. More than comfort. I need to feel something else. Something to take this pain away.

I want to run my cheek along his stubble until he takes my lips with his own. I want to run my hands up his dress shirt and feel the hard muscles I know are underneath the clothes. I want his hands on me, too. Slow and gentle, leaving goose-bumps along my skin, hardening my nipples. I breathe out steadily, but evenly. Lust clouding my judgment as I push myself harder into his embrace and close my eyes.

I imagine how he used to fuck me. He'd lay me down and cage me under him. He always watched as he entered me slowly, stretching my walls and letting me accommodate his size. But he was never gentle the whole way through. Only the beginning and then he'd lower his body and kiss my neck, my jaw, my lips as he slammed himself into me over and over. Toward the end, it seemed he lost control. I know I did.

Just for a moment, I want it more than anything. I want us both to lose control.

But I think of his words. *It's okay. You're not going to feel this way forever. I promise.*

And I know it's not true.

The whole world will go on, the sun will rise and set, and my father and I will just be *here*. As if we're frozen in place by grief, this terrible and palpable thing.

And if I don't feel this pain forever, if the feelings over-whelming me right now lessen...

Then it will truly be tragic, because a person's child should feel their loss, should mourn their death for a lifetime.

"I'm not..." I whisper into Hunter's shoulder. I pull my head back, look up at him. "I'm not okay. Nothing is... nothing is okay."

I push myself off of him, force myself to move back and forget the thoughts of him taking the pain away. I'm supposed to feel this way.

"Violet, I can't begin to imagine what you feel right now..."

"No, you can't," I snap, feeling isolated. "No one can."

"Just let me—" He reaches for me again, but I evade him, walking away a few paces.

"I can't *be* with you. I can't be with anyone right now, Hunter. I'm sorry. I'm not okay. I don't even know what okay is," I say, the words all tumbling out at once.

Hunter crosses his arms and looks at me.

"Sometimes when you're not okay, that's the moment you really need someone. You can feel it. I feel it, Vi. I don't want to lose you again."

I feel like my heart is shattering into a million pieces. I didn't think it was possible to feel any more pain, but here it is.

That is what I needed to hear him say, needed so badly four years ago. It's what I lay awake at night dreaming of, that he'd come riding in and a white horse and *save* me. From myself, from all the gossips in our town, maybe from the world.

But that was then. I draw a deep breath and exhale, my shoulders bunching.

I look Hunter dead in the eye, so there's no way he can misinterpret what I have to say.

"You never lost me, Hunter. You threw me away. There's a difference," I say, sober as a judge.

"Vi, wait," he says as I turn and start toward my apartment.

I throw one last look over my shoulder. "Goodbye, Hunter."

With that, I head toward my apartment, my bed.

CHAPTER 22

HUNTER

I haven't spoken to Violet in over a week. Not my choice. I've left her half a dozen messages. But she's not answering, I don't know if she's even seeing them. The bakery's been closed, and she's not answering her door either. I just need to know she's alright. She needs someone, and I hope she knows I'm here when she realizes that.

I lay back on the sofa as my phone pings.

I'm sure it's Jared, he's been trying to get me out of the house for the past few days, but I'm not ready to talk to anyone about this shit. I don't want a beer, I don't want to get lost in work. Not on the house I'm supposed to be fixing up, the garage I bought, not on a piece of junk car. I just… I don't know what I want.

Other than Violet.

But I can't have her. She won't take me back, and she won't let me help her. What choice do I have?

"Son," I hear my pops' gruff voice from over my shoulder and

149

I turn to him. He doesn't say anything, and neither do I. We haven't really talked since our argument.

"Yeah?" I ask him, looking straight ahead at the TV even though it's turned off.

"I know we haven't spoken much, but I thought I needed to tell you how proud I was of you."

I'm surprised by my father's words. I look over to him as he slowly takes a seat on the arm of the recliner across from me. "I mean it."

I stare into his eyes, not knowing what to say. I don't remember if my father's ever told me that before. I can't remember a time when he has. "Thank you." I don't know what else to say.

"You're a good man. It must be the way your mama raised you, 'cause God knows I have my own problems, but she raised you right. And I'm proud of the man you are." He nods his head, and I feel something shift between the two of us.

"I just wanted to make sure you knew. I love you, and I'm proud of you son."

"I love you too, Pops."

He breathes out heavily and stands up abruptly, reaching for his coat slung over the back of the recliner. I feel off-centered, that's not like my father. He's a hard man and he always has been. I can admit it's nice to hear though.

"Where are you headed?" I ask him.

"To the Shaw's. Bud left his glasses at the bar last night, I thought I'd stop by and give them to him. See how he's doing."

I nod my head and take in a slow breath. Bud is Violet's father. Before I can ask him anything or offer to go with him, I hear Haley's soft steps as she climbs down the stairs. She's careful moving around me. Everyone is.

I watch her hold onto the banister as Pops walks by and out the front door. I think about calling out to him, but I can tell Haley wants to talk by the way she's looking at me, so I don't. She's been distant since our fight, and I can't blame her.

"Hey," she says weakly, walking slowly into the room and taking a seat.

"Where's Abbi?" I ask her. She hasn't asked me to watch Abbi at all recently. Once so she could run an errand real quick. But she's been by her side and doing everything on her own. In a way, it hurts. I love being there for Abbi and for her, but I think it's doing her good to be with Abbi.

"She's still napping," she replies, but she sounds distant. "You know, when I look at her, I see Chris." Her voice chokes some, but she carries on without tears. "At first, it was hard to even look at her. She was just a reminder of him, everything was. Every little thing was just a reminder of Chris and the fact that he was gone and never coming back."

I wrap my arm around her shoulder and hold her close to me.

"I know it hurts. I'm so sorry, Haley." She lays her head on my shoulder.

"You were right, Hunter. I was trying to numb the pain, but it was only making it worse for me." She wipes at the one stray tear and pulls away from me. "Thank you." She looks me in the eyes. "Thank you, Hunter."

It takes a moment until I can find the words to say. "It's

gonna be alright. It will be, one day."

"I know," she answers and then looks at me. "You've gotta move on from what happened with Chris, too," she tells me softly, taking my hand in hers.

"It's different between you and me with Chris," I say. I feel the pain growing in my chest and squeezing my heart, but I take a deep breath and will it away. "I'm guilty in a way."

Haley's shaking her head before I'm even finished talking. "Nah, you don't understand, Haley." I have to tell her. "I was supposed to be there." I have a hard time telling her what I've been wanting to say for so long.

"If I hadn't been back on base, I could've done something. I could've tried to save them. I would've seen them coming at least."

I look into Haley's eyes with the flashes of war playing before my own. I can't stop it. I can't not see it.

We're quiet for a moment and then she says, "There are so many ifs in life. You can't do that to yourself, Hunter."

I nod my head, knowing that what she's saying is true. And I've been trying, Lord knows I have.

"You know, I told him I was fine with him going on another tour?" She gets all teary-eyed. "If I hadn't..." her voice breaks.

"No, no," I say and hold her closer as she tries to stop from crying.

"I'm sorry," she says as though it's not alright for her to cry.

"Cry all you want." I kiss the top of her head. "It's alright, Haley. It's gonna be alright. It's not your fault."

After a moment she pulls herself together and sighs deeply.

"It's not your fault either."

I let her words resonate with me.

She stares off and says, "I just loved him so much." She looks at me and says, "It hurts to think I'll never be able to tell him that again."

"I know."

She wipes under her eyes and shakes her head, sighing.

"Anyway, I just wanted to say thank you."

I give her a small, sad smile and say, "You know I love you, sis."

She huffs before replying, "Sometimes I love you, too."

I huff a small laugh.

"So what about you?" she asks. "How are things with Violet?" It's obvious that she wants to change the subject. I just wish it was to something else.

I look at her with a raised brow, but she just smiles weakly and says, "You know people talk."

I huff and lean back, not liking where things are with us.

"She's not alright. She says she doesn't want me. Which I think one day I could learn to live with. But she's hurting so bad, Haley. And she doesn't want to see me."

Haley suggests, "Maybe she just needs some time."

"I don't think she should be alone right now," I say. I don't think she wants to be alone either. She just thinks she deserves to be.

"Then go to her," Haley says.

CHAPTER 23

VIOLET

$\mathcal{J}$'m standing on the porch of my parents'... of *my dad's* house. I spent the last week in mourning, hiding out from the world. Crying, or sitting in my apartment and staring at things while trying not to cry.

Mostly I just wanted to stay out of my dad's hair. He's been wandering through the house, touching things that were my mama's. I couldn't stand to watch him, so I made myself scarce.

Today is the last day that I have nothing scheduled. I stopped by my parents'... *my dad's*... house to sort out the recycling, something that I know my father can't be bothered to do. It's something that mattered to my mama, though.

So now I'm standing outside, sorting through plastic bottles and aluminum cans. My mama used to save all the recycling up until it overflowed the bins, so now the recycling is all here, waiting for me.

It's quiet, except for the cans clinking. A couple of people have come up to give me their condolences, like ancient Miss

Juniper from down the street. She pushed her walker all the way over to my house to tell me she was sorry about my mom, and that she was a very nice person.

I just said thanks, and stared at the ground while she smiled and patted my hand. She's a sweet old lady and it was kind of her to come to me, but I don't know what to say. I don't know what they want from me. I waited until she hobbled away again, then started stacking some of the aluminum cans in the can crusher.

My fingertips tremble as I stack them. I'm barely able to grapple with the idea of my mama being gone. I keep thinking I'll turn around and she'll be right there, leaning against the doorway, asking if I want a sandwich.

I don't turn to look, though. I force my mind away from those thoughts. They aren't helping anything.

I look up from stacking cans to find Hunter's dad, Milton Graves, walking up the driveway. I clench my fist around a can.

I haven't seen or spoken to Hunter since the funeral. I've seen his texts though. They make me weak. I want to tell him yes, I need him. I want to get lost in his embrace, but I can't… if I did, there's no way I'd be able to let him go. And I know he could leave me. It would ruin me.

Late at night when I want to talk to mama, I talk to her about him. I wonder what she'd think about me going to him and giving in to the feelings that I have for him.

One of the last things she told me was to follow my heart.

Right now it's pulling me in two directions, and I don't know which to run toward. I feel like I should be in pain. And that I should hang onto it. Hunter would ease it, but for how long, I don't know. And he could cause me more pain. If he did, I don't know how I could possibly survive.

I'm too raw and fragile and I don't know that I trust him.

"Violet, how are you?" Mr. Graves says to me, stirring me from my thoughts.

His face is worn, but he looks just like Hunter. Or I suppose Hunter looks just like him.

"I'm alright, thank you," I say softly, moving the crushed cans and trying my best not to break down again.

"I'm sorry for your loss," he says and it causes me to focus back on him.

"Thank you," I tell him just like I've told everyone else.

He starts to walk past me, but then he stops and he turns to me. "You know," he starts to say and then shoves his hands in his pockets, "I remember when I lost my father. It was Vietnam."

I watch the old man talk. I've never said more than a few words to Mr. Graves. Not even when Hunter would bring me home for dinner. I'm surprised he's talking to me now.

"I'm sorry," I say the words softly. He doesn't acknowledge them, he's looking past me and down the street.

"Messed me up pretty good to lose him. My mother even more. I was young, and I remember him, but not much," he says, then scratches his face and his brows furrow. "My mom of course, she wasn't too well after that. Didn't live much longer either."

My lips part and I try to say something, but I can't. I don't know what to say, other than that I'm sorry.

"I guess what I'm trying to say is that I know it hurts," he says and finally looks at me, the same hard expression he always has, still on his face, "but time heals a lot of things."

He nods his head and doesn't wait for a response before heading inside and leaving me alone to think on what he said.

I look down at the plastic bottles and metal cans and toss the one in my hand down, not caring really where it lands.

"Violet," my body jolts as Mr. Graves' voice comes out of nowhere and scares the shit out of me. I put my hand over my racing heart.

"Sorry," he says, his forehead scrunched. "I just… I owe you an apology."

The old man surprises me again. I stand there shaking my head. He hasn't done anything wrong.

"I thought I was doing you a favor. I swear I did." He pauses and looks at the front door before looking back at me to say, "I didn't know I was splitting up something real."

CHAPTER 24

HUNTER

*S*weet Treats Bakery is sitting in front of me. I've been sitting in this truck, trying to get my ass out and moving. I was on my way to the garage, but I saw Violet's light on. She's home. It's the first time I passed the bakery and saw that she was home.

I pulled in without thinking twice, but I haven't gotten out yet. The keys are in my hands, but I wish they were sunflowers. I wish I had something for her. But I don't.

I have to try though. I'll never stop trying.

I get out of the truck and take large strides over to the side of her building where her door to the apartment is.

There's a doorbell, but I don't see it until I'm knocking my fist against the door.

I wait there, shoving my hands in my pockets and watching my breath turn to fog in the air. It's cold, winter's approaching. I take a step back and look up, the soft yellow light illuminating the windows on the second floor. She's home, and awake I'd imagine.

I take a deep breath and step forward to push the doorbell, but before I do, the door opens.

Vi's standing there in those penguin pajama pants and that same soft cream sweater I first saw her in when I came back.

Her hair's a mess and she looks tired and worn, but never more beautiful in all the times I've laid eyes on her.

"Hunter," she says my name softly and leans against the door for a second before seeming to snap out of it and push the door open wider. "You wanna come in?" she asks.

Her demeanor is different, like there's no fight left in her. I'm happy she's letting me in, but she's not alright and that's all I can see right now.

"Yeah," I say and walk in and shut the door behind me in silence.

She takes a few steps up the stairs before turning around for just a second to ask me, "You want something to drink?"

She's just going through the motions, I think. I don't answer her, I just stare up, watching her walk up the stairs until she pauses, realizing I'm not following her and she turns to look at me.

She grips the railing and looks down at her hands and then back at me. "You coming up?"

"Yeah," I answer softly and make my way up behind her. She doesn't move until my body's close to hers and then she reaches for my hand.

I clasp her hand in mine on the narrow stairway and follow

her up to the little apartment. I've never been up here. The door opens to her kitchen.

She releases my hand and walks to the cupboard, standing on her tiptoes to reach a mug.

"I hope I didn't wake you," I say, taking a seat at a tiny table across the kitchen. This place is small, but it's spotless, not a thing out of place. I wonder if that's what she's been doing, busying herself to keep her mind off things. "I know it's late."

She shakes her head, filling the mug with water and then putting it in the microwave. The beeps seem loud as she punches in the time.

"No, I was up." She finally looks back at me and I see the dark circles under her eyes. "It's been hard to sleep, you know?"

"Yeah," I say and hold her gaze. "I know it's gotta be really hard for you right now, Vi."

I almost cringe at the use of Vi. She's told me so many times not to use it, and I don't wanna make her angry. I don't wanna upset her when she's finally letting me in. But she doesn't react.

"It really is." She nods her head. "It's been really hard," her voice wavers some, but she leans back against the counter and calms herself. My fingers itch to reach out and touch her, but I stay in my seat, not wanting to ruin the little bit she's giving me.

"One of the last things she told me was to follow my heart." She talks while watching the numbers on the microwave count down for her tea. She noticeably swallows and reaches for the door before the microwave hits 0:00 and can beep.

"Your mama was a sweet lady, smart, too. She liked to yell at me some, but that's okay."

She smiles and laughs a little as she sets the mug on the counter and dips her tea bag in the hot water.

"You wanna talk about it?" I ask her, leaning forward some in my seat.

She shakes her head and picks up her mug with both hands, turning to face me but keeping her eyes on the mug. She brings it to her lips, leaning against the counter, but doesn't drink it. Instead she blows softly and finally meets my gaze. "I don't think I wanna talk."

I nod my head and say, "I get that." She takes a small sip and then another. "I'm here for you, Vi," and this time when I say her nickname, I say it deliberately. "Whatever you need, I'm here."

"I don't know what I need, though." Her words are practically whispers.

"You don't have to know, just feel."

She gives me a soft smile. "I know what I feel, Hunter," she replies as her eyes heat and her voice turns husky.

She sets the mug on the counter and stalks over to me. I'm taken aback as her small hands push against my chest and she crushes her lips to mine with a primal need, climbing into my lap. My heart beats faster as her warm curves fall into my arms and she moans into my mouth.

"Hunter," she breathes my name, breaking our kiss.

Her breasts press against my chest and I lose control, my dick instantly hardening, begging to be inside her warmth.

My hands cup her ass and then travel up her back, under her sweater.

"Vi," I say her name reverently. My eyes open as my body heats and I pull away from her slightly. Her eyes are closed and she leans forward for more, her nails softly scraping down the back of my neck. I don't give her more though. "Vi," I say, pulling back from the kiss. She opens her eyes with a look of vulnerability.

"Are you sure?" I ask her. I know she's hurting, and I don't want her to regret this. It'll kill me if she ever looks back and regrets what's between us.

She stares deep into my eyes. "I'm sure." She pauses for a moment and then adds, "I love you, Hunter," she says confidently, her hand running through my hair. My grip on her tightens, and I almost don't believe the words. "I'll love you all my life," she says as her voice goes soft and I can hear her vulnerability. "Please don't hurt me. I don't think I can take it again. My heart can't take it."

"Vi," I say and my voice is pained. I take her head in my hands and kiss her with every bit of passion I have. I pull back, breathing into the hot air between us, "Never again. I promise you. I love you, and I always will."

I stare into her blue eyes, and she stares into mine. She gives me a sad smile and leans in for a sweet kiss. It makes me feel weak. It makes my chest tighten with pain.

"Tell me you believe me," I say.

"I do, Hunter. I believe you." I can hear the sincerity in her voice.

"I love you, Vi," I say and crash my lips to hers and pull her into me so her chest is forced closer to mine. She moans into my mouth and lets her hands grip onto my back.

My heart hammers in my chest. Her warmth surrounds me.

"Please," she says in a pained voice.

"Please what?" I ask her breathlessly.

"Take it all away, Hunter," she says and sounds so weak as she opens her eyes. "Please," she whispers.

I crush my lips to hers and grip her ass in my hands as I move us to the floor. I know what she needs. I'll take all the pain away. I'll get lost in her love, and she'll be lost in my touch.

Her hands tear at my shirt, desperate to get it off. I pull it over my shoulders and toss it to the floor. She does the same with her sweater as I pull her bottoms off with her panties and shove my own pants down while on my knees. We're frantic and frenzied to get undressed. As I step out of my pants and kick them off behind me, I look down at her and see the girl I was in love with long ago.

Only now she's different.

The youthfulness is gone, replaced with the body of a woman.

I'm mesmerized by the subtle changes. My fingers linger over her soft skin. Her breathing slows and vulnerability is visible on her face. I'm quick to alleviate it.

"You're so beautiful," I whisper. Her face softens, and the trace of a smile shows before she reaches up, cupping the back of my head and pulling me down to her for a kiss.

Our tongues mix in a heated dance as my hands slowly move

down her sides and over her hips. I spread her legs for me as my tongue massages strong strokes against hers. When I cup her pussy, she's so fucking wet I have to groan into her mouth with wonder.

It's the last straw in my ability to control myself.

I line my dick up and slam into her tight heat, buried to the hilt. She gasps, breaking our kiss and arching her neck so her head is facing away from me. She's so tight. Fuck! So fucking tight. Her pussy strangles my dick, and I wait for her to get accustomed to my size.

I can't stop kissing her, I need every inch of her body touched. The need to claim her, every bit of her taking over by instinct. I leave open-mouthed kisses on her jaw, her neck, her chest as her nails dig into my back and her own back bows with the need to escape.

As soon as she takes a breath, I move and I can't stop.

I pound her hot pussy over and over. Loving how her pussy tightens around my cock, sucking me in deeper, craving more even though it's already too much for her.

My forearms brace on either side of her head as she lets out a strangled cry of pleasure mixed with the sounds of my name.

Yes!

It spurs me to go faster, harder, slamming into her, wanting to hear those sweet sounds again and again. And she gives them to me, desperately crying out my name.

Her nails claw down my back as I grip her chin in my hand and stare into her eyes, never letting up on my relentless thrusts.

My balls draw up and I know I'm going to cum, but not

without her. I need her with me. Always from now on. Always with me.

"Cum for me, Vi." Her eyes close and her mouth opens in a silent scream of ecstasy as her pussy spasms around my cock.

My head lowers and I pump short shallow thrusts into her hot pussy as the tingling grows up my spine and my toes curl. I spill myself in thick streams, filling her until our combined cum is leaking down her thighs and onto mine.

Waves of pleasure crash through me as she trembles beneath me until she's limp. Her arms fall to the ground and her head lays to the side. She's exhausted and sated, and I feel the same.

Her breathing is heavy, but slow as she pushes her hair out of her face and looks at me.

I kiss her with everything I have, as if I need her breath to stay alive.

She breaks the kiss, pushing me away with her small hands on my chest and my heart races faster with fear. But it's only so she can whisper, "I love you, Hunter."

Everything feels so right. Everything's perfect in this moment.

If only we could just stay here.

CHAPTER 25

VIOLET

I'm snuggled up tight with Hunter. The two of us are taking up my whole bed, so much so that Boots is meowing pitifully from the floor.

The side of my face is pressed against Hunter's chest. I listen to his heartbeat as we lie there, feeling really and truly loved. He's dozing, as evidenced by his deep, even breaths. My heart swells in my chest.

I can't sleep though, even as exhausted and sore as I am. I can't go to sleep without washing my face and brushing my teeth. I sigh, then rise, heading to the bathroom. Hunter stirs, but I'm not going anywhere. He's got me now, and I'm not letting him leave without a fight. He better never leave me again. The thought makes my chest hurt, but I ignore it. He promised me. He won't break it. I know he won't.

Just as I finish brushing my teeth, spitting out the toothpaste and putting my toothbrush up, there's a loud knock on my apartment door. Who the fuck? My forehead creases in confusion. It's late. There's no reason for anyone to be here.

I pad out of the bathroom, looking in on Hunter. He's awake, sitting up on his elbows, head cocked. He yawns and tries to hide it, but it only makes me smile.

He's mine.

"Probably just one of my neighbors," I say. Sometimes Mrs. Jones' cat gets loose. She lives across the street, but she always asks me to help find her cat if she's gotten out. Especially since Boots can be flirtatious with her tabby. It's gotta be her and not someone else coming to wish me condolences. It's too late for that. "Stay put."

Hunter nods, sinking back onto the bed. The knock comes again, loud and insistent. I put on my robe, running my hand through my hair to seem somewhat presentable as I walk to the door.

I open the door to find Slade standing there. My heartbeat pauses with fear, and my hand raises to my chest. He's visibly drunk, leaning to the side and leering at me.

"There you are," he says, pushing his way inside. He's slurring a bit, but he's still understandable. "I called you." I squeeze the edges of my robe tighter by my throat and take a step back, away from him.

"Slade—" I start to tell him to leave.

He reaches out and grabs one end of the sash that's keeping the robe in place, tugging on it suggestively.

"You wore this for me," he says, giving me a lascivious look up and down. "I knew you wanted me. I *knew* it."

I shrink back a step, ripping the sash out of his hand. "Slade, I don't want you. You need to leave." My voice is hard and loud.

"I don't think so," he says, moving to trap me up against the wall. "You're a little slut, you know that? Get ready to spread your legs for a *real* man."

His breath smells like straight whiskey. I squirm to get away from him, growing panicky.

"Get out, Slade," I say through my teeth. "It's over!"

"Like hell it is," he says, trying to put a hand on my breast. When I push his hand away, he growls. "Who the fuck do you think you are? You think you're too good for me? Everyone in town knows that you let Graves do whatever he wanted to you."

I grit my teeth. I want to tell him to fuck off, but I don't. "I'm never going to let you touch me like that, Slade. Get that through your thick head."

"You bitch!" Slade growls, trying to wrap his hand around my neck. My blood heats with anxiety as my hands ball into fists.

"Leave her alone," Hunter's strong voice echoes with a threat.

Slade and I both look at Hunter, who has at least put on some pants. I'm relieved as hell, but Slade is pissed. He takes a step away from me, and toward Hunter.

"Hunter, Slade, stop!" I say. Hunter is making that face at Slade, the face that says Slade is a dead man walking. "Hunter, don't," I plead with him. Not in my house. I swear to God, I can not take it.

"She's mine," Slade says, ignoring me.

"Slade, we're through!" I say, my voice rising.

Slade looks at me, a malicious smile twisting his face. "You fucking stupid bitch," he sneers.

He takes a wide step forward and throws his hands against my chest, pushing me back into the wall. I hit the wall so hard that my teeth rattle, my back slamming against the hard surface before I fall to the floor.

I'm dizzy from the impact. I almost miss Hunter swinging at Slade, almost miss the sickening crunch of bone. His fist hits Slade's face so hard that Slade goes down immediately. One punch, and the piece of shit falls limp to the ground.

"Hunter!" I say, my heart racing out of my chest.

He shakes out his fist, looking at me. "Are you alright?" His green eyes are full of concern.

"I'm okay, I think," I say, gingerly picking myself up. Hunter reaches out and helps me, taking my hand in his and bracing my body against his chest. I hold on to him and look at Slade, who's barely moving. "Is he okay?"

"Who the hell cares?" Hunter says with distaste, kicking Slade's body to check to make sure he's alive. Sure enough, Slade groans pitifully although he still doesn't move.

Slade's face is totally busted up, his nose definitely broken. There's blood all over his face, and both his eyes are already black. Yup, that nose is definitely broken.

My heart won't stop racing and I grip onto Hunter at the sounds coming from Slade's lips. I don't want him to wake up. I don't know what he'll do when he does.

Hunter pulls away from me some to cup my head in his hands, and he looks at me and then back down to Slade. "We need to call the police, Vi."

I stare back at him, with my heart clenching.

"You need to tell them everything." His gorgeous green eyes

stare into mine and my heart breaks in my chest. I know what he means, and I don't want to.

I'm terrified to. Slade's family holds a lot of power in this town. I don't know if they'll believe me.

"I'm here for you, Vi. Don't give him another chance to hurt you."

CHAPTER 26

*V*i's walking like she's going to her own execution. She keeps taking deep breaths and looking around like the world is judging her as we walk along the sidewalk headed to the police station.

Not a soul in sight is judging her. When the police showed up, she barely spoke a word, like she was afraid they wouldn't believe her even with him knocked out on the kitchen floor and me there to back up her story. She didn't wanna talk, but she did press charges.

She said if she didn't, he could do it to someone else.

Everyone knows what happened, and not a damn person is faulting her. But that's not the way she sees it, and it breaks my heart. I can't make her see things clearly, but hopefully a little time will help.

The air is bitter cold and I wanna shove my hand in my pocket, but there's no way she's gonna want me to let go of her hand. I give her a tight squeeze.

She's gotta go in to give her official statement. And then hopefully that fucker will just plead guilty so my Vi doesn't get dragged to a hearing. She doesn't even wanna talk to Sheriff Caswell, there's no way she's going to want to tell a jury what happened.

As we get closer to the glass double doors, her pace slows and I have to wrap my arm around her waist to pull her close. She pushes me away though, shaking her head and closing her eyes just a few feet from the station.

I hold her hand tighter and pull her into my side. "It's gonna be fine, Vi. You're gonna be alright."

She nods her head. "I know, I just don't like it."

"You ready?" I ask her, my hand on the doorknob.

"Yeah," she says then takes a deep breath and walks in. The warmth of the building is a relief, but it's not comforting.

The secretary behind the desk recognizes Vi and says, "You two head on around the corner," she gestures to the right side of the counter, "the sheriff's waiting for ya."

Violet squeezes my hand tighter, but she doesn't slow her pace.

As soon as we get into the office, Vi heads over to the box of tissues on the sheriff's desk. I shake his hand while he eyes her, taking a tissue and blowing her nose. It's pink and running a bit from the chill outside. She tosses it into the trash can and grabs a spare before nodding at the sheriff.

"Good to see you Violet," he says.

She gives him a weak smile and says, "You too," and finally takes the seat next to me.

"Let's make this quick," he says.

"Yes, let's," Violet says with her back straight. She's putting on a facade in front of Sheriff Caswell. I notice it, but I don't mind. If she's gotta wear her armor around other people, that's alright. She'll learn to let them in eventually. Just like she did for me.

The sheriff opens a drawer and shuffles through some papers while Violet stays stiff in her seat, I don't even know if she's breathing.

"I've written it all up, so this should be easy," he says, pulling out a folder and setting it on the desk as he leafs through it.

Finally he looks up, and seems to take notice of her.

"You're doing the right thing." Sheriff Caswell looks Vi in the eyes, but she looks down. She's got the spare tissue in her hand, but she's not crying. She's not showing her pain. She's ripping little shreds off it though.

"Thanks," she says, still looking down at the desk.

"Have you thought of anything else that you need included in the report?" he asks her, folding his hands and resting them on the desk.

Violet shakes her head and responds with a soft no, and then clears her throat and answers confidently, "No."

"Alright then, take a look at the report here," he says as he taps the stack of papers on the desk repeatedly until they're in a neat pile in his hands.

"Let me know if there's anything else you'd like to add," he says, handing her back the sheet to read through it.

She lets it sit on the desk, leaning over to see everything that's written.

I take a glance, but I don't read it all. She told me what happened, and I wanna break that motherfucker's hands. Reading it all over again is only going to piss me off.

I wrap my arm around her shoulders as she turns a page and leans into me unconsciously.

I see the sheriff give a small smile at the sight, but it's gone just as fast as it came.

She pushes the papers toward him across the table and sighs.

"It's all there."

"I'm gonna need you to sign," he says, holding out a pen for her and clicking it. "And then you are free to go, Miss Shaw."

She signs easily and breathes deep, placing the pen on top as though that finishes this chapter in her life. And I hope it does. She doesn't need this shit.

"Thank you for coming in, Violet," Sheriff Caswell says as we stand from the seats. "I'll make sure justice is served."

Vi nods her head, swallowing thickly. "Thank you, Sheriff." Her voice is confident, just like it has been, but I can see her defenses are up.

The secretary, Mrs. Summers, is standing a few feet outside the sheriff's office at a coffee machine when we walk out. I give her a nod and walk past her, but she turns to us like she's got something to say, halting us in our tracks.

She grabs Vi's wrist and hand with both of her hands and leans forward saying in a hushed voice, "I just wanted you to know, I heard what Slade did." The old lady pats the back of

Vi's hand. "I'm glad he's finally got what he's had coming to him." Vi swallows visibly and doesn't respond; she looks tense and unhappy. "You're a brave girl."

Mrs. Summers finally releases her hand and Vi takes a deep breath, then gives her a tight smile as she says, "Thank you."

"Have a good day, Mrs. Summers," I say, wrapping my arm around Vi and leading her to the front.

She doesn't breathe until I open the door to leave. I fucking hate how she's shaken up still.

"You alright, Vi?" I ask her. "You know everything's gonna be alright."

She looks up at me with wide eyes. "Yeah, I'll be alright." She leans into me and I wrap my arm around her back while I open the door.

She's gonna be alright. I'll make damn sure of it.

"Come on over to my new place with me," I say to her as we walk back to my car down the block. I don't want her staying at her apartment. I don't want to leave her alone, and I've got a lot more space at the house on the lake. I want her to see it. I can already picture her on the front porch swing, sitting next to me, right where she belongs.

She huffs a sad laugh and says, "Then I'll really be known as the harlot." I take her body language in as she holds herself defensively.

"Don't talk about yourself like that." I can't help the bite in my words. "You're nothing like that. I don't want you thinking that either."

"I'm not," she says bitterly, "that's what *they'd* say."

"Why do you let them get to you? No one thinks of you like that-" she cuts me off.

"You don't know what it was like," she says and her voice cracks. "You left me, and everyone knew what we'd done."

"They can get fucked for ever thinking any less of you. And I know for a fact, everyone I've ever met fucking loves you. They all told me I was a lucky fucker that you even gave me the time of day."

It's true. I mean every word I say.

"And they were right." I brush my thumb along her bottom lip and she parts them for me. I barely breathe the words, "I am a lucky fucker."

"I don't want them to talk about-" she whispers and I cut her off.

"They won't. I'm back now. And I'm here to stay." The hope in her eyes shines bright. "Stay with me, Vi," I pause for a moment before saying, "I love you. I've never stopped loving you."

"I love you too, Hunter," she whispers before kissing me and holding me with a force that won't be denied.

*T*onight when I make love to her, I'm gonna take my time and make sure I give her every bit of pleasure I can. It's all for her. For the rest of my life, it's all for her.

CHAPTER 27

VIOLET

I put the final finishing touches on my hair and makeup and look in the mirror, smiling. The bags under my eyes are almost completely gone, from some combination of more sleep and more happiness.

Thank God for that.

The bed groans as I sit down, slipping my shoes on. It's date night tonight, just as soon as Hunter shuts down the garage. We're going to the drive-in theater, because Hunter loves it. He says the experience is romance encapsulated.

I'm happy with pretty much anything he wants to do.

I pick a bit of lint off my bright yellow dress and sigh. The one thing that's detracting from my happiness is the situation with Slade.

The sheriff called a few minutes ago to update me. Apparently Slade pled guilty to third degree battery and public nuisance complaints. I guess he'd tried to weasel his way out of it, but the redheaded waitress from the diner told the sheriff how she had seen Slade forcing me outside and hurting me in the process. I should have been excited when the sheriff told me, but honestly I just want it to be over.

At least it's not the talk of the town, I think.

The town gossip right now is all about how I got back together with Hunter. How we were high school sweethearts, how I waited for him and only him all these years…

I roll my eyes at the busybodies in our town. They mean well, but of course they've got like eighty percent of their facts wrong.

Hunter honks the horn, which makes my lips curl up again. I grab my purse and rush out of the house, and he's there in his truck.

He gets out, looking so handsome my heart swells, and opens my door for me like a gentleman. I can't believe after all these years he's mine again.

"Hey handsome," I say.

Hunter chuckles and kisses me.

"Hey yourself," he says. He grabs my ass as I get in the truck, making me squeal. He closes my door then goes around to his side and gets in.

"Do you mind if we have a detour on the way to the drive-in?" he asks, pulling the truck out onto the road.

"I don't know," I tease. "Will there be sex on this detour?"

He glances over at me, smiling.

"We'll see."

I sit back contentedly. He drives to our old high school, which I find a little surprising.

"What are we doing here?" I ask.

He puts the truck in park, and leans over to get something out of the glove box. He drops a thick stack of letters in my lap. I remember the stack with the twine ribbon, and my heart stutters.

I look at him. "Are these... are these the letters you wrote me?"

He nods, silent. I look back down at the stack, biting my lip. I pick up the first one and start to read it aloud.

V i,

I'm so sorry that I left like I did. When I imagined leaving, that's not the way I thought it would go. I always thought...

Nevermind. It doesn't matter what I thought, does it?

What matters is what I did. I wanted to hold your hand after class and explain to you how wrong it would have been for me to keep you waiting. ...I don't think I did it right. My heart still doesn't feel alright. I wish I could go back there. With you.

I met some of the guys that will be in my unit, Xander and Chris. They seem pretty alright. At least I hope they are, because we're supposed to protect each other's asses in battle.

It's hot and sandy here, just like I expected. It's November, but the sun is blazing. No snow, that's for sure. You like the snow too much. You would hate it here.

Still, I wish I was with you. I guess... I don't know if you'll ever see this, but I should say it. Just in case.

I love you.

They're calling us to assemble now, so I'm going to go. I'll write again soon.

By the time I'm done reading, my eyes are flooded with tears. I set the letter down to swipe at my tears. I look at the date on the letter.

"It's four years ago, almost to the day," I say. I raise my eyes to Hunter. "You wrote me from the beginning."

He nods. "I had to write you. I had all these feelings... and no one to tell them to."

I don't have any more words for him. I launch myself into his arms, kissing him hard. He responds gently, kissing me back.

Eventually he pulls back, brushing my tears away with his fingers.

"This might be a stupid question, but do you want to read my letters together? I was thinking we'd read one each day," he says.

I kiss him again, although the contact is lighter this time. My heart swells in my chest, feeling like it's going to burst if I get any happier.

"That is a stupid question," I say, smiling. "Of course I want to read them with you."

"Yeah?" he asks, grinning. "Is that all?"

"Forever," I say. "I want forever along with that, too."

"Hmmm…" he says, pretending to think it over.

I laugh and smack him. He knows he's lucky to have me, just like I'm lucky to have him.

CHAPTER 28

VIOLET

"Yes!" I shout. "I mean... yes, I would like the position. When do I start?"

"Probably next week, but let me talk to the substitute art teacher first. I just wanted to be the one to tell you," Mrs. Brown says.

Thanks to Krissy, I got the job as Hallow Falls' primary school's new art teacher! I never thought it would happen.

I hold in my jubilance. "Of course. Just call me."

"I will. Congratulations, Miss Shaw."

"Thanks! Thank you so much!"

The second I hang up I let out a squeal of excitement. I can't believe that I got the job, I really can't.

I put the phone on the counter in the kitchen and take a deep breath. I look around at the new house Hunter just got. It's a little rough around the edges, and it could use a coat of paint, but I'm excited about it, too.

I bite my lip and stretch, then head to our bedroom. I step around stacks of boxes, clothes and bedroom knickknacks that have yet to be unpacked.

I throw open the closet and pull out several boxes and bags of new clothes, things I bought the day I got the call about the interview.

I check the time, and figure I have enough time to unpack some of these clothes before Hunter gets home from his brand new garage. I'm not the only one who got a new job this week.

He just signed the paperwork for the garage yesterday, and today he's there trying to figure out where to go from here.

My lips curve as I pull one bag over to the bed, opening it and spreading the contents out across the bed. I finger a black pencil skirt and a dress with a print of the cosmos.

I always wanted to dress up for work, always eyed women that had fancy jobs with envy. I thought I would be the only one in a tank and jeans every day... forever.

Now, though, I'll be one of those women I've been so jealous of. I'm going to spend a few minutes every morning carefully choosing what I will wear — because now I have the choice.

I grab another bag of nothing but cardigans, smiling like a dork. Pink and grey and leopard print, the cardigans will make sure I'm never cold. Plus, they're awesome.

"Hello?" Hunter calls from the kitchen.

I bite my lip. He's early, but you won't catch me complaining. "In here!"

I hear him trudge down the hallway, and then he comes into the room. He's wearing a tight black tee shirt and jeans, showing off his powerful arms, and he's barefoot. He gives me the same look, although I'm in sweats and a tank top. He comes over to pull me close, cupping my cheek as he kisses my lips.

"Hey," I say, pulling back. I look at him, grateful that he's in my life. I don't mean to start tearing up, but I do anyway.

He laughs at my obviously over-sentimental reaction, but not in a mean way. He understands. He always understands.

"What's all this?" he asks, nodding to the bed.

"It's just…" I start to answer, but he turns me in his arms and sweeps my hair aside, kissing my neck. "Um… clothes…"

"Clothes?" he whispers against my skin, sealing his lips over the most tender spot on my neck.

"I got the teaching job," I say distractedly. "They just… ummm… they just called."

"Mmm. I think that means you'd better celebrate," he husks. I shiver at his breath against my neck.

His hands slip underneath my tank top. When he finds that I'm without a bra, he runs his hands over my bare breasts, and we both groan quietly. I love it when he's like this, dominant and possessive and silent.

He pushes me over to the bed, leaning over me as I lay on my belly, stripping off my tank top. He pinches my nipples, getting them hard. I gasp, but he's only just started.

Hunter steps back, pulling off his shirt and unbuttoning his pants, then pulls my sweatpants off.

I bite my lip as he runs his hands over my bare ass, down to my thighs. I'm fucking wet for him, so ready for him it's ridiculous. His hand slips from my inner thigh, moving forward. He touches my pussy and growls when he finds me drenched.

He urges me onto my hands and knees. Grabbing my thighs, he pushes them apart. He pushes his pants down, then positions himself. I groan as he pushes his cock against my entrance.

"Hunter," I say and try to push him away gently. "Everyone will be here soon," I say, my words a plea. Both of our families are coming over tonight. Haley's bringing dinner so we can celebrate our first night in this house.

Hunter kisses the crook of my neck. "We can be quick," he whispers.

Not a second passes, and a hard knock at the door makes Hunter groan with disappointment. I feel awful for smiling, and a bit pissed that I'm horny as hell now, but people are arriving.

"Go let them in!" I insist, pushing him away.

"Alright, alright," he grumbles. He gives me a quick kiss. "To be continued."

He points a finger at me warningly, and I roll my eyes and shoo him away. He spends a second righting his clothes, then leaves to get the door.

I hurry to put on panties and a bra, then slip into my dress with the stars and planets on it. After a quick check in the mirror, I hurry out to the living room.

"Hey!" Haley says in greeting.

"Cookie!" Abbi shouts.

They're on the couch with Mr. and Mrs. Graves. My dad is here too, sitting on the loveseat alone. A lump forms in my throat at the sight of my dad coping without my mom, but I push it aside.

"Hey!" I say, giving everyone a quick hug. "Thanks for coming, everybody."

"Lasagna's ready," Hunter calls from the kitchen.

"Let's go sit at the dinner table," I suggest.

"Cookie! Cookie!" Abbi says, waving her arms at me.

I laugh and pick her up, carrying her into the dining room. There are boxes stacked along the wall, but at least we got the dining room unpacked. The table's all set for seven people, and I plunk Abbi down in a seat next to Haley.

"Thanks," Haley says, looking at Abbi fondly.

"Dad, why don't you sit here?" I say, pulling out a seat for him. "And Mr. and Mrs. Graves, you guys are on the end."

"Sure thing," Mrs. Graves says, her eyes sparkling. I think she's just happy that Hunter found someone.

Hunter comes in with the lasagna a second later, still hot as fire from being in the oven. He sets it down, and makes a big deal out of serving everyone. I like watching him with our families.

"I baked some bread," I say, offering the loaf to Haley.

"I should hope so," she says. "Owning the only bakery in town and all."

I make eye contact with Hunter. He nods encouragingly.

"Actually, I'm going to put the bakery up for sale," I announce. "I just got an official offer from the elementary school. I'm going to be their newest art teacher."

My dad pats my hand. "We're very proud of you."

"Thanks," I say.

"Everybody dig in, before it gets cold," Hunter says, passing the bread to his mom.

There's silence for a minute while everyone tries the lasagna, followed by murmurs of approval.

"So who are you going to sell the bakery to?" Haley asks curiously.

"I'm not sure. It's going on the market Monday," I say. "I'm probably not even going to break even on the sale, but it feels like the right thing to do."

Haley looks contemplative, but doesn't press further. She busies herself feeding Abbi, who has somehow gotten the sauce absolutely everywhere.

It's quiet for a minute. I glance around at everyone as they eat, feeling content. My dad clears his throat, then stands up.

"I'd like to say something," he says.

"Go right ahead," Hunter says.

"Thank you. I just want to say that if my beloved wife Evelyn were here, she would approve. And I think she would be glad to see us breaking bread together," he says, tears gleaming in his eyes.

"Well said," Mr. Graves says. "Hear, hear!"

I smile. We all raise our glasses to my mama's memory. I think my father was right.

My mama would approve of me and Hunter living together, and of everyone coming together to celebrate. She would approve of it very much.

I smile and eat my pasta, content.

"Krissy, it hurts," I practically seethe through my teeth as I lean back to try to breathe.

"The little stinker has his foot in your ribs, doesn't he?"

"Yes," I groan, waiting for my little man to move. He's so big, and we still have another month before he'll be here. So strong, too.

Krissy puts her hand on my belly and I can feel the slight pressure and then his little kicks. Although they hurt some, I can't help the smile that grows on my face.

Krissy's wide grin helps put me at ease, too.

"He'll be here soon, and then you'll miss this." Her eyes get a little glassy and she puts her hand on her own belly.

She's a month behind me. And her emotions are through the roof.

I look at her perfect, beautiful bump and lean back in the porch swing. The summer breeze from the lake hits my face and carries the faint smell of the laundry that's hanging on the line. It's a perfect combination that puts me at ease, and little Ryder, too.

He must've moved away from my lungs because I can finally breathe.

Krissy kicks off the ground and sends us rocking backward.

I turn to face her and say, "I can't believe you aren't going to find out ahead of time."

"I want it to be a surprise," she says as her hand rubs soothing circles on her belly.

"You're crazy." I turn away from her as the screen door opens and the guys walk out. They both have Krissy's kids, Cady and Everett, on their shoulders and they're squealing for them to go faster.

*M*y heart swells with happiness. He's been wanting a baby for a while now. Ever since he slipped the ring on my finger and made me his wife. Now that I've got the teaching job I've always wanted and Haley's taken over the bakery, I had no excuse to tell him no. Haley's a damn good baker, too. More than that, she's good with the business side of things.

Everything's perfect.

Well almost. Everything I can change. Everything I have control over.

I was hoping for a little girl. So I could name her after my mama.

Tears prick my eyes, and I brush them away. She lived a life with love and happiness. I'll do her proud by doing the same.

"Aww Vi, what's going on with you?" Hunter slips Cady off his shoulders and she runs off the steps and barrels to the field in our front yard. She's old enough to know not to go into the lake and we've told her enough times, but that little girl is a rebel and Krissy instantly stands to keep an eye on her. Jared follows behind her with Everett laughing on his shoulders and slapping his head.

They've been coming over every weekend and now that it's the summertime and school's out, it's been more often.

The swing shifts backward as Hunter sits next to me. I easily lay my head on his shoulder and sniffle.

"You alright?" he asks, rubbing his hand down my shoulder.

"Yeah," I say weakly. "You'd think after three years, it'd be easier."

"You're emotional and having a baby of your own. It's only natural." He kisses my hair and holds me as I calm myself down.

I miss my mama all the time now that I'm pregnant. I always thought I'd share this time with her. At least I have Haley and Krissy and Hunter's mom. I'm surrounded by love, and that would make her happy to know.

We swing gently back and forth and I close my eyes, just enjoying Hunter's touch. He's so good to me. We're practically the town sweethearts now... almost. I think Jared and Krissy will always have that title.

Hunter gets down on his knees and kisses my belly, wrapping his arms around me. Him holding me like this makes me feel so small, even if I am as big as a house now.

His hand rubs back and forth and he waits for Ryder to kick him, but he doesn't.

"I think he's sleeping," I say softly.

Hunter snorts a little laugh and plants another kiss on my belly and I can barely take it.

"I love you, Hunter. I love you so damn much." I don't know where my life would have gone without him in it. If he'd just given up on me instead of fighting for me.

He leans up, placing a hand on the back of the swing on either side of my head and kisses me sweetly.

"I love you too, Vi. Always have, and I always will."

The End.

If you enjoyed Promise Me, you'll love my second chance romance novel, Tell Me To Stay, available now!

Text Alerts:
US residents: Text WILLOW to 797979
UK residents: Text WWINTERS to 82228

And if you're on Facebook, join my reader group, Willow Winters' Wildflowers for special updates and lots of fun!

Hard to Love
Desperate to Touch
Tempted to Kiss
Easy to Fall

This Love Hurts

Merciless World Spin Off

It's Our Secret

Standalone Novels:
Broken
Forget Me Not

Sins and Secrets Duets:
Imperfect (Imperfect Duet book 1)
Unforgiven (Imperfect Duet book 2)

Damaged (Damaged Duet book 1)
Scarred (Damaged Duet book 2)

Willow Winters
Standalone Novels:

All I Want is a Kiss
Tell Me To Stay
Second Chance
Knocking Boots
Promise Me
Burned Promises
Forsaken, cowritten with B. B. Hamel

Collections

Don't Let Go
Deepen The Kiss
Kisses and Wishes

Valetti Crime Family Series:
Dirty Dom
His Hostage
Rough Touch
Cuffed Kiss
Bad Boy

**Highest Bidder Series,
cowritten with Lauren Landish:**
Bought
Sold
Owned
Given

**Bad Boy Standalones,
cowritten with Lauren Landish:**
Inked
Tempted
Mr. CEO

Happy reading and best wishes,

Willow Winters xx

Made in the USA
Middletown, DE
10 October 2023

40463467R00125